ANNIE'S ATTIC MYSTERIES ®

The Package

Sharon Dunn

AnniesMysteries.com

Library of Congress-in-Publication Data
The Package / by Sharon Dunn
p. cm.
I. Title
                              2010905263

AnniesMysteries.com
800-282-6643
Annie's Attic Mysteries
Series Creator: Stenhouse & Associates, Ridgefield, Connecticut
Series Editors: Ken and Janice Tate

10 11 12 13 14 | Printed in China | 10 9 8 7 6 5 4

~ 1 ~

"Here's your problem, Annie" Handyman Wally Carson pointed to exposed electrical wires in Annie's attic.

Annie braced her hand on the two-by-four of the wall frame and leaned a little closer. She gasped. "Did somebody cut the wires?"

Wally ran his fingers through his dark, curly hair. "Nah, I'd say that those wires have been chewed. See the little teeth marks?"

"Chewed." Annie repeated, comprehending what Wally was saying. "You mean mice?"

Wally nodded. "I can replace these wires, but unless you deal with your rodent issues, you'll have the same problem down the line. Next time, we might not be so lucky. They might work their way downstairs and chew through wires behind the plaster."

"That would involve ripping the walls open to do repairs." The improvements to Grey Gables, the Victorian-period house she had inherited from her grandmother, were coming along nicely. Having to tear out freshly painted walls would be a real setback.

"I would hate to see it come to that." Wally adjusted his tool belt.

"But there is no sign of mice in my kitchen. I haven't found any droppings or nibbled food." Annie glanced over at

Boots. The gray cat lifted her chin and rubbed against a box as an acknowledgment that she liked being noticed.

Wally tilted his head. "That means they must be staying up here."

"I have mice in my attic." Annie narrowed her eyes at the cat. Maybe Boots needed to spend a little more time up here.

"If they are not eating out of your kitchen, there must be something up here they are surviving on."

"You mean besides electrical wires."

The doorbell rang. Annie excused herself and rushed down the stairs with Boots trailing behind her.

Alice MacFarlane stood in the doorway, auburn red hair shining in the noonday sun. She handed Annie a brown paper bag, the petals of purple flowers were just visible above the rim. "The silk flower arrangement you ordered from Divine Décor."

Annie sighed. The last thing on her mind was a flower arrangement.

Concern etched across Alice's usually sunny expression. "Did you change your mind?"

Annie took the bag. "Oh, my, no. It's not that." She stepped to one side so Alice could come in. "I'm sure they are lovely."

Annie wandered into the living room and set the bag down on the coffee table, pulling out the flower arrangement. The living room had brightened quite a bit since she and Alice had painted the walls a sea green. She'd thought the flowers would add just the right touch.

"So what is the deal?" Alice settled in an overstuffed floral print chair. "Why are you upset?"

Annie touched the silk petals of the flowers. "Wally found out why my electricity has been on the fritz."

"And—"

"It looks like I have a mouse problem," sighed Annie.

Alice rose to her feet. "Well, I think that means I'm just in time for a mouse hunt." She hooked her arm through Annie's. "Any theories about where the little invaders might be living?"

One of the nicest things about coming back to Stony Point, Maine, after nearly thirty years had been getting reacquainted with Alice. They had played together as children when Annie spent summers with her grandmother here at Grey Gables. When Annie had returned after Gram's death, Alice had been the first to welcome her. Annie tilted her head and pointed at the ceiling. "I guess I shouldn't be so upset. How hard can it be to find a mouse ... or two?"

"Maybe it won't be so bad. You always find such interesting treasures in Betsy's attic." Now, of course, it was Annie's attic.

Leave it to Alice to look on the positive side. Annie pressed her lips together. "Somehow, I am having a hard time seeing mice as treasures."

On their way back up the stairs, Annie scooped up Boots where she rested on the landing. The door at the bottom of the stairs creaked open. Annie took the final flight back into a room filled with memories and secrets.

"If I were a mouse, where would I hide?" After setting Boots on the floor, Annie scanned the room, taking note of the dusty furniture, trunks, boxes, and stacks of magazines and books. A little light slipped in through the tiny windows.

Gram had accumulated so much in the years that she lived here with Grandpa. Where to start?

Alice rested a supportive hand on her friend's shoulder. "Maybe there is a hole somewhere, and we can just block it."

"They probably came in on another floor and worked their way up in the walls." Wally knelt on the floor by the chewed wires.

Annie shuddered at the thought of unwelcome house-guests creeping around in her walls. "We should look for a food source too." She placed her hands on her hips. "How about if each one of us takes a corner, and we work our way around the room?"

"That sounds like a good battle plan." Alice scooted across the floor toward two trunks stacked on top of each other, pushed against the wall.

Wally rose to his feet, examining the far wall, moving boxes as needed. "They've got to be here somewhere."

Annie focused on her corner, lifting boxes and checking along the wall. She brushed her hand over an antique dresser. Even though the piece was dusty and in need of refinishing, it was beautiful.

"Find something?" Alice turned toward her friend.

Annie's fingers grazed the brass drawer pulls, in need of a polish but still charming. "Gram used to have this in one of the guest bedrooms. I remember putting my clothes in it when I came up here to visit for the summer."

As a child, summers with Grandma had been something to look forward to all year long. Gram had adventures planned, from planting new things in the garden to walking the shoreline gathering treasures from the sea.

Annie opened the top drawer. "I remember lugging my big suitcase up the stairs. Gram always had the room made up so nice. I'd open the drawers and put my clothes away. She put lavender sachets in there for me." She breathed in, hoping to recapture some of the wonderful aroma she remembered from her youth, but only picked up on a musty smell. Still, the memory of wonderful scent lingered.

She regretted staying away from Grey Gables for so long. Once she'd grown up and had a family of her own, Annie had always made arrangements for Betsy to visit her in Texas, but it wasn't the same thing as coming back to the big Victorian that looked out on the ocean.

When Gram willed the house to her, Annie hadn't been sure what coming back to Stony Point, Maine, would entail. She had to admit that the short time she had been fixing up Grey Gables had done a great deal to renew her sense of purpose since the death of her husband, Wayne.

Annie clenched her teeth. And now a little mouse was going to set back all of the work she had done.

"Do you think maybe we need to move some of this furniture?"

Wally's suggestion broke through Annie's thoughts.

Annie placed her hands on her hips. The design of the dresser was such that it was flush with the floor, so she couldn't see the wall behind it. "I suppose we will have to."

"Look what I found." Alice held up a lunch box with cartoon characters on it. "I had one like this when I was a kid."

"Yes, but the question is how did Gram end up with one of them in her attic?" Annie asked.

Alice shook her head. "I think your grandmother must

have stored things for other people. I just can't picture her eating her lunch out of this."

Annie laughed at the thought. Her grandmother would have been more likely to put her lunch in a bag with one of her own cross-stitched landscapes on it. Wally moved into place on the opposite side of the dresser.

Annie hooked her hands on one end of the dresser. "Should we move on three?"

Wally swiped at the sheen of dust on top of the dresser and leaned a little closer. "This looks like maple, a heavy wood."

"I do remember it being very heavy when I got a notion in my head to rearrange the furniture in my room. Ready? One, two, three, lift." Her arms strained from the weight.

Something slapped against the wooden floor. Both Annie and Wally leaned around the high dresser to see what had fallen to the floor.

Annie knelt down beside a package wrapped in brown paper and tied with a string. "This must have been wedged between the wall and the dresser." She picked up the dusty package, turning it over in her hands. Though faded, the words *Thanks Betsy* were clearly marked in black pen.

Annie looked up at Wally who shrugged. "You got me, Annie."

She untied the string. Alice's footsteps padded across the floor. She leaned over Annie's shoulder. "Don't tell me you have found another one of your grandmother's treasures."

"I don't know." Annie carefully peeled away the tape that held the package together. The time-worn adhesive took very little effort. "Someone left this for Gram."

"A gift maybe," Alice suggested.

Stranger things had been found in attics, but Betsy had loved getting and giving gifts. Annie couldn't imagine her setting a gift aside and forgetting about it. She certainly wouldn't have been the one who brought it up to the attic.

The weathered paper crackled in her hands as she lifted it. She held her breath. On top was a folded plain piece of paper with a handwritten note. Beneath the note was a stack of papers that Annie thumbed through. They all looked the same. Printed on thick paper, they featured a swirling gold border, and the interior had a picture of a sailboat on a crystal blue ocean with calligraphy beneath it.

Alice knelt beside Annie. "I know what those are. They are stock certificates. I remember getting one from an aunt when I graduated from high school."

The stock was for Ocean Side Partners LLC, and it had been issued to someone named Therese Marie Gilkerson.

"Maybe the note is from Therese," Wally suggested.

Annie unfolded the note. The letters were rounded and precise. She read out loud. "Thanks for holding these for me, Betsy. I'll be back in a few months." The date in the corner read March 23, 1997. The note was signed simply "Joan."

Annie's mind raced a hundred miles an hour. Her palm brushed over the note. "There is a story behind this. Somebody left these with my grandmother for safekeeping and never came back for them."

"I wonder why she didn't come back. Who was this Joan person?" Wally straightened his back and adjusted his tool belt. "And why does Joan have Therese's stock certificates?"

"You think Joan stole them from Therese?" Alice's voice took on a conspiratorial tone.

Annie rose to her feet. "Gram would never knowingly participate in something like that."

Alice lowered her voice. "What if she didn't know they were stolen?"

Annie waved her free hand. "We can speculate about this until the cows come home. What we need is solid evidence. We have to find out what this Ocean Side Partners is all about and get these stock certificates back to their rightful owner."

Wally rolled his eyes. "Whoever that is."

A twinge of irritation pinched Annie's neck as she rose to her feet, still holding the package. Maybe it was fun for Alice and Wally to speculate that there was some kind of crime behind the stock certificates, but she didn't like the shadow it cast on her grandmother's good name.

"Looks like you have another mystery on your hands." Alice wrapped her arm around Annie and squeezed her friend's shoulder. "I gotta run. I'm hosting a Princessa jewelry party tonight. See you at the Hook and Needle Club tomorrow. I'll just meet you there. I've got a lot of running around to do ahead of time." Alice lived in a carriage house that was within walking distance of Grey Gables.

"You're not paying me to chitchat. I've got to get back to the shelving downstairs in the library. I am going to have to get some supplies to do a more permanent fix on that wiring." Wally headed down the stairs after Alice.

Annie stood for a moment. Clouds of dust danced in the light streaming through the tiny windows. She traced the beautiful outline of the border on the stock certificate. "Why did you have these up here, Gram, hidden away?"

~ 2 ~

few minutes before eleven o'clock on Tuesday, Annie placed a selection of crochet hooks and a brand-new skein of yellow yarn into her tote before heading over to A Stitch in Time. She put one of the stock certificates in the bag as well. Maybe the members of the Hook and Needle Club would know something about the stock certificates. She always looked forward to Tuesdays. Being with these women had added so much to her life.

Annie took the short drive to downtown Stony Point. Alice's Mustang convertible was already parked outside when she turned off Maple Street onto Main.

Annie entered the store, her feet brushing against the polished wooden floor. The store was filled to the brim with everything a creative person could desire, from fabric to yarn to scrap-booking supplies. The owner, Mary Beth Brock, was busy helping a customer select the right-sized knitting needles. The older woman offered Annie a tender smile.

Annie nodded at the other five members of the Hook and Needle Club, all seated at the front of the store. She took her usual chair beside Alice and pulled her crochet hook out of her bag.

Dressed in her pink waitress uniform, Peggy Carson looked up from the quilt block she was appliquéing and smiled at Annie knowingly. "Wally said he was over at your house doing repairs yesterday."

News traveled fast in Stony Point. Between Alice and Wally, the whole town probably knew about Annie's two mysteries: the mystery of the missing mouse house and the search for the owner of the stock certificates.

"I'm sure you have all heard by now," Annie said.

All five women nodded in unison.

Kate Stevens held her nearly completed crocheted jacket done in rich shades of burgundy and royal blue. It was nice to see Kate sitting down and relaxing instead of running around the store helping Mary Beth. "What are you going to do about them?"

Annie opened her mouth to speak but was interrupted.

"You could go see John at the bank. My husband knows quite a bit about stocks and investments." Gwendolyn Palmer sat with a ball of pink yarn in her lap, but there was no sign of her knitting needles yet. "Maybe there is some big database where he could look things up for you." Gwen's blue eyes sparkled as she spoke rapidly.

"That's an idea." Annie stared down at the yarn she had chosen to start her new project. It was a beautiful shade of yellow, but lately she had felt uninspired about her crocheting projects. She really needed something to spark her enthusiasm.

Stella Brickson let out a huff of air. The eighty-three-year-old woman sat with a straight back and slightly lifted chin as her knitting needles clicked. "If you ask me, those stock certificates need to be returned to their owner ASAP."

"That is what she intends to do," Alice said, a little short tempered.

Stella had a way of getting under people's skin with her bossy manner, but she was a faithful member of the Hook and Needle Club, and Annie felt that she was owed a degree of respect and as much love as she could offer. The older woman had spent much of her adult life living in New York. Only after the death of her husband had Stella returned to her childhood home in Stony Point.

"I think the first thing Annie needs to do is find out who this Joan person is," Peggy asserted.

Alice drew a strand of embroidery thread through her aida cloth. "Wouldn't it be easier to find Therese Marie Gilkerson since we know her last name?"

Stella stopped knitting. "I can tell you right now that there are no Gilkersons living in this area, and there never have been. I know the history of most of the families in this town and a great deal about the surrounding county."

"All last night, I was racking my brain trying to remember if Gram ever had a friend named Joan. No one named Joan came to the house when I visited in the summer. She never mentioned someone named Joan when I called her from Texas." Annie had spent the night going through old photo albums and searching through Gram's Christmas card list to see if that sparked any memory. So far, she had nothing.

"Maybe she wasn't a friend. Maybe she was just an acquaintance," Alice offered.

"Does anyone even remember if someone named Joan ever lived in Stony Point?" Peggy turned her hand sideways while she stitched, revealing red fingernails with pink flowers on them.

Mary Beth joined the group, perching herself on a chair arm.

"There was Joan who lived on Kroger Street. She owned that ugly green car that backfired all the time," Kate said.

Gwendolyn peered over her half-glasses. "That lady's name was Jo Ann."

Kate put fingers to her lips. "Oh, you are right."

Mary Beth combed her fingers through her short salt-and-pepper hair. "You know, when my mother was up at Seaside Hills Assisted Living, I remember meeting a woman named Joan. A real sweet lady. We chatted quite a bit about knitting."

"I know who you are talking about," said Kate. "She comes into the store with a group of women from Seaside Hills."

"I'll have to look into that." Annie twisted a piece of yellow yarn around her crochet hook. Yesterday she had been uncertain of what first steps she could take to return the stock to its owner, and now she had two ideas. "You ladies should open a detective agency."

"Yes, we could call it the Hook and Needle and Dagger Detective Agency." Alice raised her hands theatrically.

All of the women laughed.

Annie reached into her bag. "I brought one of the certificates for everyone to see." She passed the stock around.

Mary Beth rested her hands on her thighs. "Now that I have all of you ladies together, I have a bit of news of my own." She offered Kate a knowing glance. "It's a proposal actually."

Kate jumped in. "Mary Beth has been teaching a teen quilting class for some time now."

"The girls have just completed their big project, and the class is coming to a close." Mary Beth paused for dramatic effect. "Four of the girls have expressed interest in learning more needlecrafts."

"Oh, that sounds wonderful," Gwen said, finally taking her knitting needles out of a bag.

"Young ladies these days would do well to learn a needlecraft." Stella drew her eyebrows together to emphasize the seriousness of her comment.

"So how do we fit in?" Annie had a sense of where Mary Beth was heading.

"I just wanted to throw the opportunity out to the Hook and Needle Club—to come in for a session and teach your specialty. Even if it's a week when we don't do your specialty, you can join in and assist."

Annie's heart leapt. "That sounds like fun."

"I'm in," said Alice.

Gwendolyn nodded.

Peggy lowered her handwork. "What day is it?"

"We have been meeting on Wednesdays after school."

"I would love to help." Disappointment clouded Peggy's features. "But my boss already gives me a long lunch on Tuesday so I can come to the Hook and Needle Club. I don't think I can request more time off."

"We'll find a way to get you involved, Peggy." Annie offered as she patted Peggy's hand. "We might be able to get together for an evening once in a while."

Peggy brightened.

The women all looked toward Stella.

Without dropping a stitch, Stella said, "I think the Historical Society has some meeting planned for Wednesday."

"I'm hoping to get Vanessa involved again. She helped out with the class we did earlier, but then she lost interest." A note of sadness entered Kate's voice. "Sometimes I feel like we are drifting apart."

"She's just a teenager, Kate. You know how they are." Annie hoped her words sounded comforting to Kate. Her own daughter, LeeAnn, was grown with twins of her own, but she remembered wondering if she and LeeAnn would ever get through those teen years.

"Crocheting has been almost like therapy for me. If I could spark Vanessa's interest, I think it might bring us closer." Though Kate seemed to be mending, her divorce had taken its toll.

"That's a wonderful idea." Alice leaned closer to Kate.

"We'll get that girl coming to classes," Gwen added.

The corner of Kate's mouth turned up in a faint smile. Annie had to hand it to the Hook and Needle Club. More than once, they had lifted her spirits with their supportive nature.

Mary Beth rose from her chair. "That's enough of a commitment for me to go ahead. Our first meeting is tomorrow."

The bell on the door dinged and a customer stepped in.

"I can get this one," Kate said to Mary Beth before scurrying over to the middle-aged woman.

"I can't wait for classes to start," said Alice.

Mary Beth rose to her feet. "One thing I need to tell you ladies. Some of these girls are very well-mannered and some are … well … diamonds in the rough."

"I still can't wait," Alice added with enthusiasm.

The women finished up the meeting, chatting about upcoming events at church and in town, and working on their projects. When Annie checked her watch, an hour had flown by. As the members drifted out of the store and back to their separate lives, Annie's heart swelled with anticipation. Gram had taken the time to teach her to crochet, and it had been one of the sweetest gifts she'd ever received. The thought of being able to pass the gift on to another young lady put lightness in Annie's step as she headed out the door to the bank to talk to Gwen's husband about the stock certificates.

~ 3 ~

*T*he Stony Point Savings Bank was situated on Main Street, three buildings down from A Stitch in Time. Annie walked past The Cup & Saucer, where Peggy was already back at work. She passed the public library and pushed open the doors of the bank. John Palmer was seated behind his desk, talking with an older woman dressed in a bright red coat.

John made eye contact with Annie. He waved as though he was expecting her. Gwen might have called ahead.

He passed a single sheet of paper across the desk to the older woman, stood up and leaned over his desk to point out several things to her, and then excused himself while the woman filled out what must have been an application of some sort.

John tugged on his tie as he approached Annie.

"Did Gwen call you?"

"She filled me in," John said.

"I brought one of the certificates." She pulled her purse out of the tote where she kept her crocheting and then pulled out the padded envelope in which she had carefully placed one of the stock certificates. "I counted the certificates. There are fifty of them."

John examined the paper. "So someone bought fifty shares of Ocean Side Partners LLC."

"Do you know who they are?"

"I can tell you they never got a loan through this bank or incorporated in this town. Ocean Side Partners could be in another town or another state."

Annie fought off the desire to give into defeat. This was only her first stop. "So you don't know what kind of business they are?"

John shook his head.

Annie tensed. Now came the big question. "Why would someone named Joan have Therese's stock certificates? Did she steal them?"

"I doubt it. These days most stock purchases are all done electronically. The only reason to do the fancy-paper stock certificate would be because it was intended as a gift or maybe this Therese person wanted something concrete for repayment of a debt."

Annie breathed a sigh of relief. Of course Gram wouldn't have been party to a theft. She kicked herself mentally for even allowing the thought into her head. "So maybe Joan bought the stock intending to give it to Therese?"

The woman in the red raincoat rose from her chair and made her way toward John. "I've got to take care of this customer." He offered the customer a smile and then turned back toward Annie. "I wish you luck with your search."

Annie carefully placed the stock back in the envelope. When she stepped out onto Main Street, the gathering dark clouds promised rain. Alice had said that spring in Maine usually meant lots of rain and thunderstorms; so far they had been very lucky with weather. Maybe their luck wouldn't hold any longer.

Annie zipped up her light jacket and headed across the street to Malone's Hardware. Wally had suggested she go in to see what was available to stain the new shelving in the library. When Annie stepped into the store, Mike was in the process of pricing terra-cotta planters, looking as fit as ever for a man in his fifties.

"Hey there." He waved his pricing gun at her.

"Wally wants me to make a decision about what kind of stain to put on that shelving in my library."

Mike ran his hands through thinning hair. "I set aside some samples for you." He sauntered over to the checkout and grabbed a stack of 2-inch wood samples bound together, each with a different kind of stain.

She filed through the samples. The stains ranged from almost translucent, allowing the natural grain of the wood to come through, to dark. It was a small decision, but sometimes she felt there were just too many choices. "Well ... um."

Mike's thin mustache twitched. "If you are anything like my Fiona, you can't make a decision on the spot. Take the samples home and think about it."

"Thanks. You read my mind." She stuffed the samples in her tote.

When she stepped outside, the streets that had been bustling with people were virtually abandoned. Only a few lost souls scurried to get out of the rain—some with umbrellas and others shielding themselves with newspapers or whatever was at hand. This wasn't like the dry weather in Texas. She needed to get into the habit of bringing an umbrella with her.

Even though she tried to stay under the awnings that some of the downtown businesses provided, she was soaked by the time she got back to A Stitch in Time where she had parked her car.

A warm glow came from inside Mary Beth's store. Kate looked up from the receipts she was sorting and waved at Annie.

Wet and a little chilled, Annie slipped behind the wheel of her Malibu and headed back to Grey Gables. Her windshield wipers squeaked out a rhythmic pattern as she made her way down the hill. She pulled into the driveway. After grabbing her bag, she ran up the driveway to the porch. Boots was perched on the doormat. The cat let out a plaintive cry, complaining of the inconvenience she had been through.

Annie stopped. Something was wrong here. Boots had been resting on a pillow on the couch when she left this morning. Her heartbeat accelerated as she checked her front door. Still locked.

"How did you get outside?"

Annie gathered the forlorn-looking feline into her arms. Balancing cat, keys, and bag, she managed to get the door open. Boots sprang out of her hands and trotted past the dining room into the kitchen to her food dish.

She set her bag on the counter and put the kettle on. Tea would warm her up. Except for the crunching sounds of Boots filling her belly, the house was still.

All the same, a tingling started at the back of Annie's neck and snaked down her back. She shivered.

She checked the back door. It was still locked as well.

When she surveyed the living room and dining room, nothing looked out of place. Her chest felt tight. She couldn't shake the feeling that someone had been in her house.

She raced up the stairs. The few pieces of valuable jewelry were still in the cedar box Wayne had given her on their first wedding anniversary. The money she kept on her nightstand, a few dollars and a china cup filled with loose change, had not been touched.

Carefully she opened the bureau drawer and made sure the stock certificates were still underneath the sweaters where she had left them.

She stood for a moment, lost in thought.

The whistling teakettle made her jump.

She ran back down the stairs and pulled the kettle off the burner. Boots had settled on her plush cat bed in the kitchen.

While the tea steeped, Annie checked the desk drawers in the living room. She couldn't remember the arrangement of paper clips and receipts, but nothing looked out of place. Still uneasy, she wandered into the kitchen to get her tea and then back to the front room.

Annie sipped her tea and stared out at the ocean view. Waves crashed against rock. Only a single brave fishing boat remained on the tumultuous water. This storm was probably going to last into the evening. It would be a perfect day to sit in her plush chair and get started on her crochet project. While she worked, she could think through how she would instruct the teen girls tomorrow.

She turned back around to face the quiet living room. Again, the tingling started at the nape of her neck.

She needed to let go of the idea that someone had been

in her house. Maybe it was just the thought of mice scurrying through her walls that made her feel she wasn't alone.

She inhaled the steam rising from her teacup and then sipped. The minty flavor lingered on her tongue.

The only problem with the explanation for her uneasiness was that mice usually didn't open the door and let the cat out.

— 4 —

The next morning the rain had let up, but everything, including the flowers Annie had planted, was damp and battered. The poor little violets looked like they'd taken a beating. Maybe they would recover. The lawn, which had just started to turn green, was saturated and muddy. She wouldn't be going outside today to work on the yard.

The sound of the rain spattering against roof and windows had helped her fall asleep the night before. Old houses had a life of their own. Annie had grown used to creaking sounds and the sudden blast and tingling of pipes as the heater kicked on. The rain, though, had acted like a lullaby that drowned out any possibility of hearing mouse noises.

She spent the morning organizing bills for the construction and repair supplies Wally had purchased. When she got a chance, she'd take them down to Malone's. After straightening up the house, she sat down at her desk in the living room to look through decorating magazines for ideas. The lights blinked off and on. Before she could even think about the library, this electrical problem needed to be dealt with. The mice must be chewing on wires that connected into certain rooms, because it was never the whole house that went dark.

She called Wally to verify that he would be able to come by later to finish fixing the electrical problem in the attic and discuss what she had planned for the library. Wally said that he had a job that would take most of the day, but that he could swing by before he went home. At two o'clock, she put on a slow-cooker meal of chicken stew with dumplings and ate a late lunch. She called Alice to see if she would be around to go to A Stitch in Time for the afternoon class.

Alice's chirpy voice vibrated across the phone line. "I am knee-deep in doing orders for Divine Décor, but I am still planning on coming. I'll pick you up."

Annie changed out of the jogging suit she'd worn through the morning and put on a skirt in a bright spring pattern, a camisole, and a matching lacy cardigan she had crocheted. She touched the lightweight cotton yarn on the sleeve. The cardigan, a series of crocheted flowers, had been one of her most successful projects. It was so very different from Kate's heavy jackets. Maybe wearing it would inspire the girls about what they could do with a crochet hook and a little imagination. She ran a comb through her blond-gray hair, selected a pair of green earrings to match her eyes, and applied some lip gloss and mascara.

By the time she got back downstairs, the kitchen was swirling with the scent of basil, rosemary, and tarragon from the slow cooker.

Annie slipped an umbrella into her bag just as the doorbell rang. Alice looked fresh and springy in her purple raincoat. As they drove into town, Annie felt a mixture of excitement and anxiety. She remembered Mary Beth's warning that some of the girls were diamonds in the rough. Though she had never thought of herself as a teacher, she liked the idea of getting a young person excited about crocheting.

When Annie and Alice stepped into the store, Kate was behind the counter. Two middle-aged women pulled out bolts of fabric and draped them over their shoulders.

Mary Beth, sitting at the front of the store with three girls, offered Annie a little wave.

Annie's stomach flip-flopped. Ready or not, it was time for the lesson. She stalled by talking to Kate. "Did Vanessa come?"

Kate shook her head. "She said she would come for the knitting lesson. She's always said that she likes that I crochet." Kate dropped her gaze. "I think she's intimidated by the projects she's seen me do. I wouldn't expect her to crochet like a pro off the bat."

Annie patted Kate's hand. "She'll come around. You are going to be a part of the lesson, aren't you? You are the most gifted crocheter I know."

Kate smiled and tilted her head toward the two women picking out fabric. "I'll join you as soon as I can."

Annie's nerves kicked into high gear at the thought of having to do the lesson by herself. She hoped the store wouldn't be too busy and Kate could help.

"Let's go." Alice urged Annie on.

The phone rang, and Kate walked to the counter to get it.

Now the butterflies in Annie's tummy were going crazy. She glanced at the three girls. A petite blonde sprang to her feet. She held out a hand. "Hi, I'm Lily, and I already know how to crochet."

"Then you can help the other girls," Mary Beth suggested. A tinge of tension threaded through her voice.

Lily lifted her chin slightly. "If they let me help them." Precise French braids framed Lily's narrow face.

Kate joined the group but didn't sit down. "Gwen just called. John sprang a last-minute dinner party on her for some important bank customers, so she has to get ready for that. She felt bad, but she promised she would do everything she could to be here for the other lessons." Kate returned to helping customers.

Great, now it's just me and Alice.

A girl in a cheerleading uniform let out a huff of air, crossed her arms, and looked at the ceiling.

"This is Mackenzie." Mary Beth put her hands together in an gesture of ambiguity.

Mackenzie's wavy brown hair fell softly around her heart-shaped face. She was a pretty girl with bright brown eyes and clear skin.

"Mom made me come," Mackenzie said. "I am only here so Erin would feel comfortable about coming." Mackenzie leaned toward the girl sitting next to her.

"And this is Erin." Mary Beth placed a hand on the shoulder of the third girl.

Erin bent her head so far forward that her straight brown hair covered most of her face. As though she was balancing a ball on top of her head, she craned her neck slowly and offered Annie and Alice the faintest of smiles.

Something in Erin's expression tugged at Annie's heart. Like a turtle going back into her shell, Erin bent her head again and stared at her hot-pink canvas high-tops. Except for the shoes, Erin was dressed in brown and beige. Wearing the shoes seemed like an act of bravery on Erin's part.

"We are expecting one more girl." Mary Beth glanced toward the store entrance.

A girl whose most prominent feature was her purple lipstick and black hair entered the store and made a beeline for the group. "I'm here."

"And this is Taylor," said Mary Beth.

Taylor patted her chest with her palm. "Sorry, I am out of breath. I rode my bike over." Taylor had a beautiful smile.

Lily sat with her back as straight as a board, turned slightly sideways in the chair with her hands folded in her lap. "My mother dropped me off in her new Cadillac."

"Who cares how you got here?" Mackenzie narrowed her eyes at Lily, who drew her mouth into a straight, hard line.

Mary Beth cleared her throat as though trying to get rid of some of the tension that had entered the room. "And this is Alice and Annie. Annie is going to get us started with crocheting today."

"And I do cross-stitch. But I will help out as much as I can with the other lessons," said Alice.

"Each of the girls made a lap quilt for the last class, so I thought we would start by showing off their projects." Mary Beth indicated a far wall where four quilts had been hung.

Annie walked over to the displayed quilts. The first quilt was done in yellow solids and prints in a Log Cabin design. Though the quilt was well pieced and stitched, there was something mechanical about it, as though the designer had followed directions exactly but made only safe choices. The second quilt was simple: nine blocks in red, white, and blue solids and prints. On closer examination, Annie saw that the patriotic quilt had no hand stitching. The machine stitching looked hurried and imprecise, as though the quilter had made up the design as she sewed. The third quilt looked almost antique in its design and fabric. The quilter had not gone with safe color choices, though everything seemed to blend. Pastel blues, rose shades, tan, gray, and just a touch of green all came together beautifully. The effect was calming, like a quiet spring day. The final piece was a crazy quilt done in animal prints. Though the stitching was uneven and coming undone in some places, there was something daring and inspired about the quilt.

"I have an idea." Taylor, who hadn't sat down since she arrived, bounced from foot to foot. "How about you guys guess who did which quilt?"

Alice raised a playful eyebrow toward Annie. "I'm game."

Annie nodded.

"OK, quilt number one." Taylor pointed at the yellow quilt and hummed a game-show theme.

Annie and Alice looked at each other and said in unison. "Lily."

Taylor made a positive "you're right" game-show noise. "Now quilt number two."

Alice whispered in Annie's ear. "Erin?"

Annie studied the patriotic quilt. "I think it is her sister's."

Alice nodded in agreement and then said, "Mackenzie."

This time Lily and Mary Beth joined in on making the "you're right" noise. Everyone laughed.

"And now quilt number three."

"Erin," Annie blurted.

"I agree," said Alice.

Taylor made a "you're wrong" game-show noise. "I knew you were going to think I did the animal print crazy quilt."

Annie hadn't noticed it at first, but Taylor had emerald-green eyes. Under the purple lipstick and dark eye shadow was a very pretty girl. Her enthusiasm was infectious.

Annie walked over to the crazy quilt. "Erin, you did this one?"

Erin lifted her head and nodded. "I know it's not very good."

Part of Annie had wanted Erin to be the one with the quilting gift. Maybe that was why she had thought the quiet girl had done the quilt that demonstrated the most natural ability. Annie touched the crazy quilt. "Erin, I think this is inspired."

The compliment caused color to rise in Erin's cheeks.

Annie studied the last two quilts again. She'd made assumptions about people based on first impressions. Did the designs indicate the artists' emotional state, not who they were on the outside? Taylor, despite an initial impression of being a rebel, connected with people and seemed to have an inner confidence, and quiet Erin was a crazy quilt done in animal prints with unraveling stitches.

Kate came and stood behind Mackenzie's chair. "Looks like I am just in time for the lesson."

"Ladies, get your hooks out," commanded Taylor.

"All the girls have already picked out a crochet hook and yarn," Mary Beth said.

Taylor's good humor seemed to lighten the mood of the girls a great deal.

Annie looked up at Kate. "How should we do this?"

"Why don't I start crocheting and talk the girls through it, and you and Alice can go around to any girl who needs help?"

"I won't need any help," Lily chirped. "My mother taught me how to crochet."

"How long are we going to spend on this, anyway?" Mackenzie slumped in her seat.

"I thought we would go through week by week and just kind of sample crocheting, knitting, and cross-stitch, and then if there is something you really like, you can select a bigger project."

"Those quilts were fun, but I wish we could do a project that was something different from making stuff for ourselves." Taylor finally took a seat. She pulled a crochet hook and yarn from her backpack.

"You mean like do something for the community?" Lily pulled a ball of green yarn from the bag beside her. "Maybe make some things and sell them to raise money for a charity."

"That's a great idea, Lily," Kate said.

"The cheerleading squad and the football team could use extra funds," Mackenzie added.

"What about the school band?" suggested Lily. "I play the flute, and this year we are planning a trip to a big competition in Portland."

The bell for the store door dinged. "I'll get this one, Kate." Mary Beth rose from her chair and made her way across the store as several women came in.

"We'd have to come up with something that we all could agree on," Taylor added.

Kate lifted her crochet hook. "Just keep brainstorming. I'm sure we will think of a good project. Are we ready to start the lesson?"

Annie took a seat beside Erin.

Kate lifted her crochet hook and slowly talked the girls through making a slipknot and beginning stitches. The girls followed her lead, creating a foundation chain.

Erin leaned close to Annie and whispered. "Did you make your cardigan?"

"Yes, and Kate makes some of the most beautiful jackets." Annie pointed to the one on display in the store.

Erin mouthed the word, "Wow."

"When are we going to be able to do stuff like that?" Lily sat her project on her lap. "This is baby stuff."

"Slow down, Lily," Kate said. "Just like with the quilting, you have to learn to walk before you can run."

A haughty tone entered Lily's voice. "I already know how to walk."

Mackenzie held up her chain. "I don't think your stitches look any better than mine, and I just learned."

"Mine are more even," Lily blasted back.

"I think I am getting the hang of this," said Taylor.

The girls held up their chains. Erin's was about half the length of the other girls'. Each stitch had been a struggle for her.

"I have clumsy fingers." Erin focused so intently on the yarn and hook that a crease formed between her eyebrows.

"You're doing just fine," Annie encouraged.

"I'm not blind." Erin's voice carried a tinge of pain. "I know it's not that good."

Alice divided her attention between Mackenzie and Taylor, who both seemed to be picking up on Kate's instruction.

"Lily, you might want to slow down," Kate suggested.

"This is so boring. I know what I am doing. I want to start on a sweater. Mom said she would buy me the materials. Can I go see what you have?"

"You are always welcome to look around," Kate said.

Kate progressed to teaching the girls a popcorn stitch, and then she asked Annie if she wanted to take over.

Annie talked the girls through several more stitches.

Taylor held up her sample. "So what do we do with this?"

"These are just practice stitches. Once you feel you have the hang of everything, you might want to think about a simple project that incorporates some of the stitches. A scarf is usually a good choice."

The girls continued to work and banter for the rest of the hour.

At a quarter to five, Erin and Mackenzie's mother came to pick them up. Lily's mother arrived a few minutes later. Lily and her mother stayed in the store while Lily filled a basket with things she needed for her project.

Annie and Alice stood on the sidewalk while Taylor unlocked her bike. Annie stared at the darkening sky. "It's starting to cloud up. We could give you a ride."

Taylor smiled. A sparkle entered her green eyes. "I'll be OK. I like riding in the rain." She swung her leg over her bike, pedaled a few feet, and then stopped. "I had fun today."

"We did too," Annie said.

Alice nodded in agreement.

While they watched Taylor pedal over the hill, Lily came out holding a bag heaping with yarn.

Lily shook her head. "I feel so sorry for Taylor. She has

to ride her bike everywhere. She has like a billion brothers and sisters, and her mom and dad just have one old car. You know what I mean?"

Alice's mouth formed a tight line. "She didn't seem too bothered by having to ride her bike, Lily."

Annie was impressed by her friend's restraint. Lily had a way of getting under everyone's skin.

Lily's mother emerged from the store, zipping her purse shut as she stepped through the door. She was dressed in a coordinated jogging suit. Her brown hair was cut short and curled under.

"This is my mom, Karen Parker."

"Are you the ladies who taught the class today?"

Alice and Annie nodded.

"Lily has been talking about this all week. She was so excited," Karen said.

"Mom," Lily objected.

Karen raised a scolding eyebrow toward her daughter. "Lily, I'm talking. I am delighted that Mary Beth offers something like this. I tried to teach Lily the basics, but I reached the end of my expertise pretty quickly."

Lily rolled her eyes, but remained silent.

"We're glad to help," smiled Annie.

"Come on, Lily; we need to go home and get dinner on the table for your father."

Mother and daughter crossed the street and got into their car.

Annie watched the car pull away from the curb. "Interesting. Lily has been looking forward to the class all week. I couldn't tell that from the way she acted."

Alice crossed her arms over her chest. "Maybe she likes the class but pretends not to."

"Sometimes kids hide who they really are. She only talked about doing things with her mother. Maybe Lily doesn't have lots of friends. This is her chance to be with other girls her age," Annie said.

"She isn't exactly putting in a lot of effort to be a friend," Alice pointed out.

"Which is all the more reason she needs to be in this class." Annie glanced at her watch. "I need to get home. The electricity is still on the blink. Wally said he could stop by late in the day before he went home."

Annie and Alice headed back toward Grey Gables. When Annie got out of the car, Wally was standing on the steps. Annie slowed her step. An older man with white fluffy hair stood beside Wally.

~5~

nnie scurried up the walkway, flipping open her purse and digging for her house keys. "Wally, I am so sorry. I totally lost track of time." Annie stepped onto the porch and turned the key in the lock.

"It's all right, Annie We just got here a few minutes ago, and I misplaced the key you loaned me." Wally pointed to the white-haired man. "This is Douglas Emery. He's an electrician. In addition to our chewed wires, I noticed some electrical issues in the library. I thought I'd let Douglas have a look."

Annie nodded toward Douglas as she opened the door. And she had thought she would just fix some shelving and add extra outlets in the library. "Everything is always more involved than you think it is going to be when it comes to construction, isn't it?"

"We'll just have a look today. I won't start on anything until I give you an estimate."

"Thank you. You are the best," Annie said.

"Library is over this way." Wally led Douglas down the hall and disappeared around the corner.

Annie headed down the hall into the kitchen. She checked on the slow cooker. Spices wafted through the kitchen when she lifted the lid. She stared down into the pot. Even if she froze some of this, she'd be eating it for weeks. A sliver of pain pierced her heart. Learning how to cook for one person was just one more adjustment she had to make with Wayne gone. She closed her eyes for a moment, seeing Wayne smiling at her with the crinkles in the corners of his gray eyes. She breathed deeply to shake off the sadness.

The chicken could probably stand to cook a little longer. Annie leaned against the counter, Boots swirling around her legs. She was just thinking she should mix up some juice to go with her meal when the phone rang.

Annie picked up. "Hello."

"Annie, it's Peggy. Is Wally there?"

"Yes."

"It seems my husband forgot to charge his cell phone again. Can you please tell him to swing by the store on the way home and get some cream of mushroom soup?"

Peggy sounded tired. "Sure, I'll let him know. Did you have a long day today?"

Peggy let out a sigh. "I'll say. My feet are killing me. I was sure I had one more can of that soup left in the pantry. I was going to make a casserole. We'll just eat late."

"Actually, I think I can solve your problem. I made a chicken dish. I don't know what gets into me. I made enough to feed a small army. I can send some home with Wally."

"You have no idea what a blessing that would be. I have been looking at food all day at work. The last thing I want to think about is fixing dinner."

"I understand. When Wayne and I worked at the dealership all day, sometimes a nice, simple sandwich sounded like the best thing in the world."

"So, did you have the first class for the teens today?"

"Yes, there were four girls. All of them very ... different. I think it went well."

"I wish I could help out. I love kids that age. I always thought if Wally and I could ever scrape the money together, I would go to college to be a junior high teacher."

"I wish you could be there too." Annie could hear the longing in Peggy's voice. "Maybe it will work out some Wednesday for you to come."

"I doubt it. I either have to work that shift or the dinner-to-close shift, which would mean I would have to find someone to watch Emily."

"It's never easy, is it?"

"You got that right. Thanks again for sending the dinner over. I owe you one. And please tell that husband of mine that his phone is not working."

Annie laughed. "I'll let him know." She hung up and turned away from the window she'd been staring out. Douglas walked past the kitchen. Wally must have sent him on an errand.

She unplugged her cooker and opened the cupboard where she kept her plastic containers. While she spooned the stew into the container, Douglas ambled past the kitchen holding electrician's tape and a plastic box that looked like a meter of some sort.

"Everything going OK?"

"As good as can be expected." Douglas rubbed the white stubble on his cheek. "This wiring is ancient. If it were me, I would gut out the whole place and start from scratch."

An involuntary gasp escaped Annie's lips. "I don't have the finances to do that."

Douglas disappeared around the corner.

Annie searched the cupboards for a plastic cover to go with the container she'd filled. A few minutes later, Wally and Douglas poked their heads in the kitchen.

Annie handed Wally the container with the stew. "Your wife called. Dinner is on me tonight. But you do need to charge your cell phone."

Wally slammed the heel of his hand against his forehead. "Not again."

"Did you take care of the electrical problem in the attic?" Annie asked hopefully.

"Yes, we did find some mouse droppings, so for sure this isn't just because of frayed wires," Wally said.

Annie groaned. "I have put out an all-points bulletin for those mice, believe me."

Douglas touched his white fuzzy head. "Mice love to use insulation to make a house." "It's just a matter of time before their destruction spreads."

Annie was growing weary of all of the doomsday predictions about the mice. Wally and Douglas made it sound like Grey Gables would be a pile of sawdust in no time at all. "I'm sure we will find them before it gets that bad. I've been so busy. I'll spend some time looking for them tonight."

After Douglas and Wally left, she ate a quick dinner and raced up to the attic to look for the mice again. Annie pushed open the door to the attic and walked up the creaking stairs. Though it was only a little past six o'clock, the sky had already turned a soft gray. She clicked on the single light, an incandescent bulb that hung in the middle of the room, and studied the dark corners. The little bit of light was not going to be enough to find her evasive rodents.

She retrieved a flashlight from her bedroom. Boots followed her up the attic stairs.

"When are you going to start doing your job?"

Boots didn't respond.

Annie surveyed the attic space, promising herself that she would not get distracted by looking through Gram's treasures. Besides, she already had the stock certificates to deal with. Everything in this room told a story, and every item revealed more about Gram. If Gram had not known this Joan person well enough to ever mention her, how had they known each other? Joan had trusted Gram enough to give her the package.

Annie decided to start in the corner where they had moved the antique dresser. Finding the package had distracted her from her search. She swept the flashlight over the area. Boxes were stacked on top of one another, and she noticed a broken doll crib. A mouse might nest in a box.

She moved several boxes, looking inside each one. She opened a small trunk, closed it, and pushed it away from the wall. Nothing. Annie stood back to study the area again from a different angle. Silence blanketed the room. She took in a breath of musty air.

Across the room, a box crashed to the floor. Annie jumped and her heart skipped into double time. Boots scooted out from behind the box.

She shook her head at the cat and picked up the contents of the box, mostly old magazines. As she set things back in order, an old wooden box that advertised peaches caught her eye. Annie reached over and picked it up, but put the box down almost immediately when she saw what was behind it. A long fabric tube, like the ones used to keep out a draft underneath a door, caught her eye. The tube had been chewed in several places, revealing that it was filled with rice, a tasty treat for a mouse. Now she was getting somewhere.

Trying to keep more rice from falling out, she gathered up the tube and placed it in the wooden box. Enough rice was scattered across the floor to warrant getting a broom. She had just closed the door to the attic at the base of the stairs when the doorbell rang. Annie set the box on the landing and headed toward the front door.

She opened the door and Alice offered her a bright smile. "I have to deliver a Princessa jewelry order up to Seaside Hills Assisted Living, and on a lark I thought I would see if you wanted to come and talk to that Joan lady that Mary Beth said she knew."

"Sure." Annie checked her watch. Peggy was probably done with dinner by now. "Let's call Peggy and see if she wants to meet us there. I think she is feeling kind of left out."

"That's a great idea." Alice opened her purse and pulled out her cell. "I can call her right now."

"Let me grab my coat and the sample stock certificate."

The sky had darkened even more by the time Annie and Alice got into Alice's Mustang.

Alice turned the key in the ignition, and the car roared to life. "Peggy said she would meet us there. She's bringing Emily."

All day long the air had felt thick with the promise of rain, though none had fallen. Annie was starting to think that the rule about spring in Maine was to be ready for rain anytime. She was adjusting to the change in weather, though the cold breeze off the ocean often made her feel she had a permanent chill underneath her skin. Fortunately, the bathroom at the end of the hall featured a deep claw-foot tub to soak in at the end of the day.

They drove across town past the bank and turned onto Elm Street. The Mustang hugged the curving road up to Seaside. Annie pushed open the door and breathed in the salt air. She walked to the edge of the parking lot. The night view of town lights and the ocean beyond stirred up her heart. Gram had done dozens of cross-stitch landscapes of different settings around Stony Point but never the view from this hill. Sorrow flooded through Annie as she thought about all of the works of art her grandmother could have made. The body of work for Betsy Originals was substantial, but still, how wonderful it would have been to have more days with Gram.

Thinking about her summer visits, she could picture her and Gram coming up here, Gram with her sketch pad and she with a book or crochet project. Always, when she had gone with her grandmother, she ended up watching her sketch, entranced by the focused eye of an artist as her gaze went from canvas to landscape.

Alice placed a hand on Annie's shoulder. "Some memories turning in that head of yours?"

Annie nodded.

"I miss her too." Alice said as Annie turned back around.

Peggy waved at them from across the lot. Emily held onto her mother's hand while holding a doll in the other hand. Annie was used to seeing Peggy in her waitress uniform with her hair pulled back. The effect of the quilted jacket done in shades of blue and Peggy's short dark hair framing her face made her look quite stylish.

Emily rocked back and forth, heel to toe. "Come on, Mama, let's go."

"She loves coming here," Peggy said. "Her first-grade class has been doing a volunteer project where they come up every Tuesday afternoon."

"I get to read stories to my friend Elizabeth. She says she's a movie star," Emily drew her eyebrows together, her expression growing serious. "But Mama says she's just pretending."

The foursome stepped through the glass doors into an expansive foyer that featured a huge Oriental rug done in shades of green and gold.

"I'm going to go find Elizabeth." Emily bounced, waiting for her mother's OK.

"All right, sweetie, but ask the nurse first if Elizabeth wants to have visitors."

"I will." Emily gleefully scooted around a corner and disappeared.

They stepped into a solarium containing numerous lamps and soft couches and plush chairs. The lighting was subdued and warm.

Alice pointed to the bag she held that had the Princessa jewelry logo on it. "I'll be right back. My client is expecting me."

Annie looked to Peggy. "I am not sure where to start. I don't even know Joan's last name."

Peggy pointed to a woman behind a counter flipping through papers on a clipboard. "She looks official."

The woman couldn't have been a day past twenty-five, and she offered Peggy and Annie a wide smile as they approached. "Hi, I'm Katrina, the activities director."

"We are looking for someone," Annie said. "Her first name is Joan, and we know that she likes to go to A Stitch in Time to buy supplies."

"You must be talking about Joan McTavish; she's quite an avid knitter. I think I saw her come into the solarium a few minutes ago. May I ask why you want to talk to her?"

Annie explained about finding the stock certificates and the note from Joan.

"That seems benign enough." Katrina came out from behind the counter. "Forgive me for being nosy. Sometimes relatives come in to ask for money or pick a fight over something that happened twenty years ago. I feel a little protective toward the residents."

"I understand," said Annie.

Katrina led them across the carpet to a woman sitting in a chair beneath a lamp.

"Joan, these ladies would like to have a word with you."

Joan looked up from her knitting. She was a round woman with steel-gray hair cut close to her head and large wire-rimmed glasses. She rose from her chair and strode toward them.

Annie's heart skipped into double time. Maybe this was the mysterious Joan. She introduced herself and then Peggy. "I'm so sorry to take you away from your knitting."

"It's quite all right." Joan's trilling voice reminded Annie of a songbird.

A tightness entered Annie's voice as she realized she

might finally get some answers. "The reason we wanted to talk to you is to ask you if you know anything about this." Annie pulled the stock certificate out of the envelope.

Joan's eyes lit up, and a tiny bit of hope crept into Annie's heart. Joan took the certificate. Her face glowed as she studied the piece of paper. "Oh my, it is just beautiful. This isn't mine though. Look, see, the name here."

"It came with a note that was signed with the name Joan."

"Oh really." Joan held the stock certificate out at arm's length as though she were trying to remember something.

"We found it in Betsy Holden's attic. Did you know her?"

"Of course I knew her. Everybody knew Betsy."

"So did you give my grandmother a package with these stock certificates?"

Joan's arm dropped. "I'm sorry. I knew Betsy, but we weren't close. I knew who she was. We said hello on the street. I've never been to her house."

Annie felt like a balloon losing air. "So you didn't leave a package with her for safekeeping?"

Joan shook her head. "I'm so sorry, dear."

Alice entered the room from the far side. Her energetic stride slowed when Annie looked in her direction.

"No luck, huh?" Alice said as she neared.

Peggy shook her head.

"Would you dears excuse me?" Joan smiled. "I have a project to get back to."

Annie stared around the solarium. A woman in the corner sat under a lamp sewing a button on a jacket. Across the room, another woman was busy with a cross-stitch in a hoop. With the exception of two knitters who sat across from each other, no one was interacting with anyone else.

"Maybe this trip wasn't for nothing," Annie said as hope returned.

"What do you mean?" Alice leaned closer to her friend.

"Look around; this is a senior citizen Hook and Needle Club." Annie pointed at each of the different women working on projects. "They just don't know it. Alice, do you remember how Taylor said she wished they could do a project that wasn't just about making something for herself?"

"You mean the seniors and the teens do a project together?" Alice brightened.

"I bet Katrina could help us organize it." Peggy sounded excited. "We could plan some evening meetings, so I could come and help."

"I have an even better idea." Alice shifted her weight. "The hospital accepts donations of little knitted and crocheted hats for newborns."

Annie grabbed her friend's hand. "The seniors and the teens could get together and make a whole layette."

"I have a client who works in labor and delivery at the hospital. I can talk to her." Alice checked her watch. "She might be off duty tonight. I can swing by her place and run the idea by her."

Annie's mind raced. "Peggy and I can broach the idea with Katrina tonight, and then we will see if the teen girls will go for it."

"I can give you a ride home," Peggy offered.

A few minutes later, Peggy and Annie hunted down Katrina as Alice sailed out the door, promising to let them know how her talk went with her friend from the hospital. Katrina's eyes grew wide as Annie shared her idea.

"You know, some of those ladies used to sit together in a sewing circle. After the unofficial leader passed away, they all just sort of drifted apart. I'll get started on talking to them to see what the level of interest is."

Peggy retrieved Emily from her visit with Elizabeth, and the threesome headed toward the foyer.

"Wouldn't it be wonderful if we could pull all this together: three generations of women giving to the new generation entering the Stony Point community?"

Peggy looped her arm into Annie's. "It's coming together pretty fast. Now you just have to get the teens excited about it."

Annie pushed the doors open, and they stepped out into the dark, clear night. She thought of each of the girls who came to the class. "Yes, that is one challenge we face."

~6~

$\mathcal{P}$eggy dropped Annie off and waited in the driveway with the headlights on until Annie was safely inside. She had decided to crochet a newborn's jacket with the yellow yarn she had bought. The girls might be excited about working with the seniors when they saw what they could do with their skills. She grabbed her crochet hook and yarn, and headed up to the master bedroom, which had a comfortable chair with good light. Annie worked on the little jacket until she felt her eyelids getting heavy. She let the project rest in her lap and leaned back in the chair, slowly drifting off to sleep after she clicked off the floor lamp.

She awoke with a start in total darkness. She couldn't see the glowing numbers of the alarm clock from where she sat. Had the electricity gone out again? Her heart pounded out an intense rhythm when she detected scratching sounds above her. Sweat trickled down Annie's back. She leaned forward, fumbling for the light, but as she knocked against it, the lamp crashed to the floor.

The scratching sounds grew louder, more intense. Still half asleep, Annie scrambled across the room toward the main light switch. When she clicked it, light filled the room. Good, she had electricity.

She let out the breath she had been holding. Now to deal with the scratching noises. It had to be coming from the attic. Could mice make that much noise? Annie stepped out of the bedroom and headed toward the landing where she had left the box with the draft blocker filled with rice.

Now the scratching was accompanied by a plaintive meow. "Oh, Boots." Annie scrambled toward the attic door at the bottom of the stairs. She opened the door and the cat burst toward her, rubbing against her leg and complaining profusely. "You poor thing." Annie gathered the cat into her arms. "Did you get hungry and kill some mice?"

Annie took Boots into the bedroom and settled her on her favorite cushion. She glanced around the room. The noise and the darkness had stirred her up. The memory returned—of feeling like someone had been in her house. The noises had just been Boots's desperate attempt to escape, but still she felt vulnerable. Annie opened the drawer where she'd put the stack of stock certificates. She pulled a box out of her closet that contained yarn and crochet patterns and books. She pulled out most of the yarn and placed the stock certificates in the bottom of the box, pushed the box to the back of the closet, and placed several pairs of shoes on it.

She sighed. It had been a long day, filled with both disappointment and renewed hope. The prospect of doing something that would make her feel like an integral part of the Stony Point community buoyed her up. Fatigue settled into her muscles, and she slipped beneath the soft comforter. Boots crawled onto the bed beside her and purred. She hoped there wouldn't be any more scratching noises in the night.

*   *   *   *

The week went by in a whirl of activity. Wally and Douglas came by a few afternoons to work on the library. Only one section of plaster had to be removed to replace some old wiring. Annie ran errands when needed. She brought home paint samples, hoping to match the color that was already on the library wall. In the end, she decided she'd just repaint the whole thing. So far, there didn't seem to be any further problems with the electricity. Now that she had found the food source for her unwelcome guests, maybe they would skedaddle.

Alice phoned to say that her friend who worked in labor and delivery at the hospital was enthusiastic about such a big donation. Annie worked on the yellow infant jacket. If she could get most of it done by Wednesday, the girls might be inspired and get excited about the intergenerational project.

Tuesday morning, Annie put the nearly complete yellow jacket in her bag and headed over to A Stitch in Time. All of the women but Peggy had already taken their usual chairs.

Gwendolyn looked up from her knitting. "Alice just told us about your idea."

"I think it sounds wonderful," Kate added.

"What do you have planned for tomorrow's lesson?" Gwen adjusted her glasses and held a knitting pattern at arm's length.

"Cross-stitch," said Alice. "That means I'm on board to teach."

"And then for the week after that, we'll go through some basic knitting," Mary Beth stood outside the circle of chairs watching the door for customers. "By then, each of the girls may want to choose a project doing whatever she likes best."

"I am definitely coming for that." Gwen's knitting needles clicked at a rapid pace. "I haven't done much cross-stitching, Alice. You might be teaching me."

"You should come anyway. Get to know the girls." Annie laid the little yellow jacket on her lap.

"I have to admit," said Alice. "I'm a little nervous. They can be a tough crowd."

"I wonder," mused Annie, "if they would like to see some of the cross-stitch work my grandmother did."

"That is a great idea, Annie." Mary Beth crossed her arms over her chest. "I could talk forever about Betsy Originals and what an artist she was, but seeing her work makes all the difference."

"What those girls really need is inspiration." Alice cut off a piece of brown embroidery thread with her little scissors. "We need to get them excited about being creative."

Peggy slipped into her chair and pulled out the appliqué quilt square she had been working on. "Sorry, got caught up in a rush at work."

As usual, Stella sat up very straight in her chair focused on her knitting. The older woman always added a sort of regal presence and dignity to the group.

"You know, when Wayne and I were so busy at the Chevy dealership because we were doing a big sales push, the thing that got me through the day was thinking about working on a project, just sitting alone in my chair at night in the quiet."

Peggy pulled out several different quilt pieces. "I know what you mean. I love thinking about color combinations with my quilts, coming up with something new that hasn't been done before. Sometimes at night I dream about fabric."

"Oh, I do that too," said Kate. "Only with me, it's different stitch combinations and blending different kinds of yarn."

All the women laughed.

"Dreaming about yarn. Well, I never!" Stella huffed, but the corners of her mouth turned up in amusement.

"Speaking of color combinations—" Peggy held up two fabric pieces cut into diamond shapes. "I'm piecing a new quilt. Do you think these two colors go together?"

Gwendolyn leaned forward and narrowed her eyes. "They both have teal in them."

"I like them together. If you paired them with a solid in a shade of green, it would work," Mary Beth offered.

Peggy looked at her samples again. "That's what I was thinking, and then maybe I can find another solid to complement the yellow in the prints."

While the other women chatted, Annie focused on finishing the sleeve on her jacket. The jacket was coming together nicely. She could just picture the sweet newborn who would wear it.

Gwen's voice broke through Annie's thoughts. "So you hit a dead end with finding your elusive Joan?"

Annie nodded.

"Do you even know if the stock is worth anything?" Kate asked.

"I need to find out what Ocean Side Partners is first," Annie said. "I just haven't had time to get over to the library, and my laptop is on the fritz."

"What if they are out of business, and you can't find them at all?" Peggy smoothed over her quilt block.

"Which would make the stock worth nothing." Stella arched an eyebrow.

That thought had crossed Annie's mind too. "I still feel like I should make an effort to return the stock to its owner."

Annie checked the clock. It was nearly time to go. The hour had flown by.

Peggy rose to her feet. "Let me know how tomorrow's class goes."

Gwen and Stella had already packed up their bags.

"We have a pot-roast special at The Cup & Saucer if anyone is interested." Peggy picked up her fabric squares and hiked the straps of her supply bag on her shoulder. "I gotta run."

Annie's mouth watered. Fresh pot roast sounded way better than leftover chicken. Wally and Douglas were probably back out at the house banging hammers, not exactly a pleasant atmosphere to eat or crochet in. "I'm in," said Annie.

"I've got another party to get ready for," Alice moaned. "And I need to think about the best way to get teenage girls excited about cross-stitch."

"You'll do great," said Mary Beth.

After saying her goodbye, Annie stepped out onto the sidewalk and headed one door down to The Cup & Saucer. When she stepped inside the little restaurant, Peggy was already taking an order at a table. The aroma of rosemary and basil swirled in the air. Annie scanned the room feeling a rising disappointment. The tables were full.

A man waved at her from a corner table. Ian Butler, the

mayor of Stony Point, indicated an empty chair at his table. Annie made her way through the crowd. Ian was dressed casually in khakis and a light blue button-down shirt.

Annie took the chair Ian offered her. "Thanks, I had my stomach all set on pot roast." She noticed his empty plate. "You've already eaten."

"I've got blueberry pie coming." Ian patted his lean stomach. "I saved just enough room."

Peggy appeared at their table with two plates. She set the pot roast in front of Annie and winked. "I saw you come in." She set a dessert plate of pie with a dollop of ice cream in front of Ian. "And for you, sir."

Ian rubbed his hands together before picking up his fork. "Thanks, Peggy."

"Best service in town." Annie savored the richness of her first bite of beef in gravy. The meat was so tender it pulled apart with her fork.

"Can't beat the Tuesday specials," Ian commented between bites.

"Cooking for myself isn't exactly fun."

A sadness crossed Ian's expression and the sparkle in his eyes dulled. "I know what you mean." Like Annie, Ian had lost a spouse suddenly.

Annie's heart went out to this sweet man. "Thank goodness we can come and eat at The Cup & Saucer." She tried to sound upbeat, but a chord of sorrow had struck inside her as well.

Ian managed a smile. "So I understand you found something interesting in Betsy's attic, again. I talked to John from the bank the other day."

Annie nodded. No surprise that Ian had heard. News traveled faster than a rocket ship in Stony Point. "I think I am going to have to give up on this one. I can't find anyone named Joan who left the package with Gram. And this Therese Gilkerson could live in Timbuktu for all I know."

"Joan?" Ian placed a forkful of pie in his mouth and chewed.

"The note was left over a dozen years ago. Nobody remembers a Joan who lived around here at that time."

Ian crosshatched a design in his ice cream with his fork. "What if she didn't live here? What if she was just visiting?"

Annie sat up a little straighter. "That would explain why I don't remember Gram having a friend named Joan. Maybe she was someone visiting Gram from out of town."

Ian shook his head. "There may have been a Joan visiting at that time, but I would have remembered if she had stayed with Betsy. She must have been visiting someone else." He tapped his fingers on his forehead. "Let me ask around and rack my brain a little bit."

"Thank you, Ian." Annie draped her hand over Ian's, feeling a spark of warmth. "I was ready to give up."

Peggy appeared at their table and placed a glass of water in front of Annie. "Forgot about that." She straightened her back and placed her order pad in her apron. "So, Ian, did Annie tell you about our plan to get three generations of women in Stony Point to work together on a project?"

Ian lifted his head a little higher. "Really, I love anything that builds community in Stony Point."

Annie's cheeks warmed. "It's just in the planning stages right now."

"But it is going to be fabulous. Tell him, Annie. I gotta go. A customer is waving at me." Peggy darted to the other side of the room.

Ian leaned toward her. "I'm all ears."

"It wasn't just my idea. Alice and Peggy helped. We are trying to get the teens in Mary Beth's class to work with the seniors to make some layette sets for the newborns at the hospital. Of course, the Hook and Needle Club would help out."

Ian's expression brightened. "That is a great idea. What a positive thing to do for the community. You might be from Texas, Annie, but you are thinking like a true Stony Point native."

Ian's compliment warmed her heart. "Really?"

"So are you planning a big ceremony when you present the gifts to the hospital?"

"I ... I ... um ... really hadn't thought that far ahead."

"I can help you set something up." Ian wiped his mouth with the cloth napkin. "Mike Malone has taken on a high school student as a reporter for *The Point*. The kid is a pretty good photographer too."

"Should we really make such a big deal about it?"

"It's great PR for Stony Point. Please, let me see what I can put into place."

Annie took a sip of water for her dry throat. This project was growing bigger and more involved by the minute. She hoped she hadn't bitten off more than she could chew. "Everything is still kind of tentative."

"I understand." Ian rose to his feet. "Just keep me in the loop. And I'll let you know if anything jars in this old noggin about this Joan person." He snatched up Annie's meal ticket, which Peggy had just left on the table. "I got this."

Annie watched as Ian ambled through the restaurant, stopping to greet people and shake hands. As he paid the bill, Ian said something that made the woman behind the cash register throw back her head and laugh. If there was anyone who was proud of his town, it was Ian Butler. Ian turned and offered Annie a wave before disappearing through the doors of The Cup & Saucer.

Annie finished the last few bites of her pot roast and then headed down the street to Malone's, to pick up supplies Wally had requested and pay her bills. She had just left the store when her cell phone rang.

"Wally here. Look, I'm tied up on this other job and won't be able to get over to your place."

Annie opened the door to her Malibu. "That's all right. I understand." A quiet afternoon at home would be nice for a change. The hammering and the scraping and the sawing had to happen, but she had been seriously thinking about going to the public library to work on her crochet project for her own peace of mind.

Rain spattered lightly against her windshield as she drove home. Grabbing her umbrella and her bag, she raced up to the porch. The supplies she bought would just have to wait. She burst through her door shaking out the umbrella.

Boots trotted toward her and wailed. The cat was insistent in her meows as though Annie would understand exactly what she was saying. After putting away her coat and umbrella, Annie stepped into the living room. Her skin tingled. She walked over to the desk. A tiny gasp escaped her lips.

The drawer to the desk was open an inch or so—not as though someone had been sloppy but in a hurry. Slowly, she slid the drawer open; the contents looked jostled. A votive candle had been knocked to the floor. Boots may have knocked the candle over, but she couldn't open drawers.

Annie's heart hammered as she scanned the room. Nothing else looked out of place, but the drawer was enough.

She raced up the stairs. When she opened her bureau drawers, she saw that the sweaters had been moved from where she remembered.

Annie dropped to her knees and reached to the back of the closet. She pulled shoes off the box and slid the box across the carpet. She held her breath as she lifted the lid and dug down through the yarn. Her fingers brushed over the soft paper the stock certificates were printed on.

That settled it. She was putting these certificates in a safe-deposit box. She took the certificates downstairs and got the final one out of her purse. Once they were all together in an envelope—and she had counted them to make sure there were fifty—she called the chief of police to let him know she suspected a break-in. As she had expected, no report could be filed because it didn't look like anything had been taken or any damage done. Chief Edwards was sympathetic and promised that a patrol car would go by Grey Gables tonight.

She wrapped the envelope containing the stock certificates in a plastic bag, grabbed her umbrella, and headed out the door. Once on the porch, she jiggled the doorknob to make sure it was locked. She'd been in such a hurry when she'd come home, she couldn't remember if she had taken her keys out and unlocked the door or not.

Annie set the envelope on the passenger seat. Her hands were shaking as she turned the key in the ignition. She inhaled deeply to calm herself. The rain was falling hard by the time she turned off Maple onto Main Street. She rounded the hill and stared in the rearview mirror. A dark blue van followed close behind her. There was no parking close to the bank, so she circled the block.

She found a space around the corner. The rain had cleared most of the people off the sidewalk. Juggling the waterproof package in one hand and her umbrella in the other, she made her way up the sidewalk. Footsteps echoed behind her. When she turned to see who was following her, only two older gentlemen shuffled along. Yet the footsteps had sounded strong and energetic.

Annie quickened her pace. No matter how many deep breaths she took, she couldn't calm her nerves. She pushed through the bank doors. Several people craned their necks in her direction. John Palmer wasn't behind his desk.

She approached a red-headed bank teller. "Can I help you?" The teller smiled and laced her fingers together.

Annie pressed the package against her chest. "I need to get a safe-deposit box."

The teller's expression clouded with concern. "Are you all right? Your hands are shaking."

"I guess ... I was just ... spooked."

"I should say." The teller grabbed a single sheet of paper and skirted out from behind the counter. "Come right this way. Have a seat here and fill out this application. We will need an initial payment."

As she listened to the swirling of her pen across the paper, Annie calmed. The certificates would be safe here. Her pen hovered above the paper. What if it wasn't the certificates the thief was after? She shook her head. It had to be. She couldn't think of anything else of value worth breaking into her house for. Whoever had broken into the house thought the certificates were worth something.

If she could just find Ocean Side Partners, she would know for sure.

The teller led Annie into a windowless roomed filled with a wall of metal boxes. Annie placed the certificates in the bottom of the box. She'd be glad when these could be returned to their owner.

She thanked the teller and left the bank. When she checked the rearview mirror, the same van she had seen before was behind her. Annie zigzagged through town, taking the long way home. When she checked her rearview mirror again, no one was behind her.

A knot of tension had formed at the back of her neck by the time she finally unlocked the door and stepped into the living room of Grey Gables. She pressed her back against the door and stared at the ceiling. She didn't need to face this alone.

She picked up the phone and called Alice. As she explained what had happened, a tear warmed her eyelids.

Alice was sympathetic. "How are you doing?"

"To be honest, I am really shaken up by the whole thing."

"How about I come over? We can make popcorn and watch a movie."

Annie sighed with relief. "What would I do without

you, Alice? Bring your cross-stitch. I've just got to put the finishing touches on my infant jacket. We can work on our projects together."

Ten minutes later, Alice rang the doorbell. Annie found a black-and-white Grace Kelly film on the classic movie channel. They munched on popcorn while Alice talked about her ideas for the class.

"I know I can find some photographs of a Betsy Original and pictures from the magazines she was featured in. I can bring the Betsy Original that I have. All those girls have probably seen the landscape of Butler's Lighthouse that is hanging in the public library," Annie added.

They both worked on their projects into the evening until Alice yawned. Annie hugged her friend at the door. "Thank you."

"Tomorrow is the big day," Alice commented as she flipped open her umbrella.

Annie watched from the porch while Alice made her way down the stairs and along the path to the carriage house. Annie stood for a moment with her arms crossed, listening to the rain patter on the roof of the porch.

She slipped inside Grey Gables, sliding the dead bolt on the front door and double-checking to make sure it was locked.

~ 7 ~

Annie pulled up outside A Stitch in Time ten minutes before the teen class was set to start. She gathered together the envelopes that contained photographs of Gram's designs and magazine clippings featuring her work.

Gwendolyn came up the sidewalk. "Can I give you a hand?"

Annie handed her the envelopes. She leaned back in the car to grab the framed original from Grey Gables. Inside the store, Alice had already found a seat. Both Kate and Mary Beth were waiting on customers. Mary Beth offered Annie a welcoming smile.

As Kate made her way back to the cash register, Annie asked. "Is Vanessa coming today?"

"I don't think so, but I keep hoping."

"She'll come around." Annie smiled before making her way to the circle. She leaned the print against the wall.

Alice studied the cross-stitched picture of jagged rocks of the Maine coastline. "That really is one of her most striking pieces, isn't it?"

"It's always been one of my favorites."

"What if we create a sense of drama by covering it with some fabric and then revealing it at the right moment?" Alice's shoulders hunched up in excitement.

"That's a great idea," said Annie.

"I think Mary Beth has some scrap fabric in that box." Alice pointed toward a shelf.

Annie found a calico print that would be big enough. "Should we tell them about the project with seniors before we start the lesson?"

Alice pulled a stack of cross-stitch projects in hoops out of her bag. "I hope they go for it."

Annie stared at the pile of hoops in her friend's lap. "Alice, are those all unfinished projects?"

"Yes, I am a little A.D.D. when it comes to starting projects. The exciting part is when I first get the supplies and think about how great the project is going to be, and then reality sets in—I realize how much work it is going to be."

Annie laughed. She had seen enough of her friend's completed projects to know that many of them indeed made it into a frame. "Everyone has a different style, don't they? I can't start a second project until I have completed the first."

Gwen stood behind a chair. "My weakness is buying supplies. I have so much yarn that I had to buy a bureau just to store it. I keep telling myself that I can't buy more yarn until I use up some of what I have, but then I see a beautiful color, and I can't help myself."

The doorbell dinged, and Taylor entered the store, followed by Lily. A few minutes later, Mackenzie with Erin trailing behind her came through the door. All of the girls settled into their chairs, each with a hoop and aida cloth and a selection of thread. Lily had already started on her project. The girls looked up at Alice expectantly.

"Before we get started with the lesson, we have

something we would like to share." Alice couldn't hide the excitement in her voice. She looked toward Annie.

Annie felt a little flutter in her stomach as she spoke. "Last week, Taylor mentioned that it would be neat to do a project that wasn't just about making something for yourselves."

Taylor nodded, her eyes growing wider. Erin leaned forward, showing interest.

Annie took in a deep breath. Maybe this would all come together.

"We were at the assisted-living place on Elm Street a few nights ago, and Annie got the most wonderful idea." Now Annie understood why Alice was so good at her job. Her enthusiasm would convince an Alaskan that she needed air-conditioning.

As Annie explained the project to the girls, Taylor was the only one who visibly offered a positive response.

Annie laced her fingers together. "So what does everyone think?"

Mackenzie crossed her arms. "Would this mean it would take more of my time?"

"We haven't worked everything out, but we might have an evening or afternoon up at Seaside, and the older women could maybe come here during your class."

"I think that would be nice," said Erin.

Lily made a sucking-on-lemons face. "Those old-people places smell funny." She fanned herself. "They are always so hot."

Annie tried to hide her disappointment with a smile. "Well, you girls think about it."

As Alice started her lesson, Annie found herself thinking about how much work had already been done on the project to get things lined up. None of that mattered if the girls weren't interested.

Alice talked about Gram and her work. When Alice looked in Annie's direction, she rose from her chair and pulled the fabric from the Betsy Original. The heavy silence as the girls studied the work of art was the best part of the lesson so far.

Even Mackenzie's mouth dropped open. "Wow—that's really awesome!"

Annie began passing around the photos and magazine clippings she had brought along.

Alice proceeded with her instruction, and then each of the girls held up the simple pattern she had chosen and started her own work. The chatter died down as the girls pulled embroidery thread through aida cloth.

"Why do we have to do such small projects?" Lily asked.

"I like making Christmas ornaments." Erin didn't look up from her project. "Uh-oh, I have a knot."

Annie set down beside Erin. The entire back of her cross-stitch was knots.

"I'm not doing an ornament. I'm doing a pincushion for my mom." Lily held up her project. "Aren't these violets pretty? It's going to take me like ten seconds to do this. Why can't we do something bigger?"

"We just thought we would give you a sample of each of the needlecrafts, and then if there is something you really take to, you can do a larger project." Alice tried to cover her impatience with Lily, but Annie picked up on it.

"Do you think we will ever be as good as your grandma?" It was the first time Annie had seen Mackenzie show interest in needlecraft.

"She worked for years to perfect her skill. It is certainly something to aspire to."

Even as sadness about the girls' lack of response to the community idea settled in, Annie felt a little morsel of joy. Maybe the day was worth it just to see a baby step forward for Mackenzie.

Erin leaned close and whispered to Annie. "It's not very good, is it?"

"Cross-stitch isn't for everyone." Annie tried to sound encouraging.

Erin's shoulders slumped. "But I'm not good at anything."

Annie wrapped an arm across Erin's back and squeezed her shoulder. "That is not true. Sometimes it just takes a while to find what you do best."

Gwen sat next to Lily. She studied the pattern and then looked at Lily's project. "I think you have an extra row in your leaf."

"No, I don't," Lily snapped as she lifted her chin.

"Oh," said Gwen, a bit stunned. "I'll just set the pattern here, and you can look at it when you like." Gwen scooted away from Lily as though she were a yapping poodle.

The lesson finished up, and the girls trailed out the door. Taylor was the last to leave. She shoved her hands in the pockets of her baggy black pants.

"Did you ride your bike again, Taylor?" Alice sorted through the pile of projects she had brought as examples.

"No, my mom had to take my little sisters to the library.

I'm meeting them down there." She strode toward the door but turned back around. "Just for the record, I like the idea about working with the senior citizens."

"Thanks for your vote of confidence," Annie said. No one had outright said no. Maybe the girls would change their minds after they have had a week to think about it.

Taylor ambled out the door after hiking her backpack onto her shoulders.

After the door closed, Annie buried her face in her hands. "One step forward and two steps back. I didn't think they would be over the moon with the idea, but I hadn't counted on that kind of response."

Mary Beth placed a skein of yarn on a machine that rolled it into a ball. "One thing I learned from teaching the quilting classes: Sometimes what you see on the outside with teenagers is the exact opposite of what is happening inside."

"I can attest to that with Vanessa." Kate folded a fabric remnant. "I think they are programmed to act indifferent about everything."

"Maybe we shouldn't attempt something so big and involved." Annie gathered up the photographs of Gram's projects. "We'll just teach them the basics and quit trying to be so ambitious."

"I don't think we should give up so easily." Mary Beth's voice took on a singsong quality.

"What are you thinking?" Alice strode across the store.

Mary Beth's eyes sparkled. "These girls barely know each other, and they certainly don't know us. We need to do something that shows them we have their best interest in mind."

"You mean like some sort of get-together?" Alice asked.

Mary Beth walked across the store and stepped behind the counter. She pulled a purple flyer out from under the counter. "I got the idea when I saw Mackenzie's eyes light up for the first time when she saw that Betsy Original."

The women gravitated toward the counter like moths toward light.

"Kate and I were just going to go up to Four Corners by ourselves because I have a booth there for the store, but ..." She flipped over the flyer.

Annie read out loud. "Largest needlecraft fair in New England."

Kate stood beside Mary Beth. "It's way bigger than the one we did at Stony Point a while back."

"It's a bit of a drive, but I think the girls would have fun," Mary Beth said.

"We can't get them to commit to something here in town," said Gwendolyn. "How are we going to talk them into this?"

"I think it's worth a try. Regardless, it sounds like a fun day. We could all go even if the teens don't want to," Alice said.

Mary Beth smoothed her hand over the flyer. "What do you say, ladies? Each one of us can call a girl and invite her. We'll meet here Sunday after church and carpool."

"I'll call Erin and Mackenzie." Even as they talked, Annie's spirits lifted. "Let's just see what happens. The girls would get to know us in a different context, and they might be inspired by what they see."

"I'll call Taylor," Alice piped up, "and let Peggy know what the plan is."

"I guess I get Lily." Gwen picked up her large handbag.

"And I think we should call Stella too. She'll probably say no, but I don't want her to feel left out."

"I have to go up on Saturday to set up, but Kate will be here at the store."

Annie took in a deep breath. "It's settled then. We'll encourage the girls to come and meet here at ten thirty on Sunday."

~ 8 ~

On Sunday at 10:25, Annie pulled up outside A Stitch in Time. Eager to get to the store, she'd kept her church clothes on: a blue skirt, denim jacket, and crisp white shirt. The store was closed on Sunday, but a single light revealed that Kate was inside working on something behind the counter.

Annie tapped on the glass. Kate waved and worked her way toward the door. She slipped outside. "Just wanted to use the time to catch up on some things."

Gwendolyn pulled up at the same time that Peggy and Alice came around the corner in Alice's Mustang.

The women gathered on the sidewalk, watching the street.

"So here we all are." Gwendolyn rocked back and forth on her heels.

"This will be fun even if it is just us." Alice's enthusiasm sounded forced.

"Think positive thoughts," Annie added.

"This will be my first chance to meet these girls." Peggy opened her purse. "I brought a camera."

Alice pulled a camera out of her purse as well. She looked toward Gwendolyn. "Is Stella coming?"

Gwen shook her head.

All of the women stood up a little straighter when a car slowed as it went by. A single passenger, a man, was visible as the car approached.

"How long should we wait?" Gwendolyn pulled a compact out of her stylish leather purse and redid her lipstick.

"I think Taylor will come. We should at least wait for her." Annie hoped she was wrong. She wanted all of the girls to come. Erin had actually sounded like she had wanted to come when Annie invited her over the phone, but if her older sister wasn't interested, Erin probably wouldn't show.

"Let's give them fifteen minutes," Kate said.

Annie tilted her head. The sky was a gorgeous robin's egg blue with no sign of dark clouds. A perfect day. Annie closed her eyes and enjoyed the cooling spring breeze. She opened her eyes when she heard a car pull to the curb on the other side of the street by the hardware store.

Lily got out of the passenger side of the car. Annie decided to ignore the look of total boredom that Lily managed to wear most of the time. The girl was here. That's what mattered.

Lily crossed the street and stood in line with the other women.

"I like your skirt," said Gwen.

Lily did a little curtsy. Annie detected just the faintest brightening in her features. "Thank you; I made it myself." Lily quickly returned to the scowl she wore like an accessory and cleared her throat. "I hope this is fun. I could have stayed home and helped my mom make sugar cookies."

A car parked across the street. Mackenzie got out of the passenger side, and a moment later Erin emerged from the back of the car.

Kate leaned toward Annie and whispered, "People surprise me all the time."

"Me too." Annie's heart fluttered. "It's good to be surprised."

A moment later another car arrived and parked half a block down the street. The rear door opened and Taylor appeared. A baby toy fell out onto the sidewalk. Taylor bent down to pick it up and tossed it back in the car. When she leaned into the passenger side window to say something to her mother, a pair of tiny arms and a blond head appeared to give her a hug.

Annie could discern at least three other children in the car.

Taylor wore black pants and a teal shirt that brought out the green in her eyes. Around her neck was a crocheted scarf in shades of green.

"You made that?" Annie touched the soft eyelash yarn.

Taylor's easy smile was infectious. "Yeah, I went a little crazy and stayed up half the night. It was kinda fun."

Alice clapped her hands together. "Well, ladies, shall we hit the road?"

"My van can hold seven," said Kate. "I think we can all fit in two cars."

Gwen offered to be the other chauffeur. The women and teens piled into the two vehicles. Though Four Corners was more than a hundred miles away, the time went quickly. Gwen played an instrumental CD that no one objected to. Annie got out a project to start on, an infant hat to match the jacket. She hadn't given up hope yet.

She noticed that Mackenzie had brought along the cross-stitch ornament to work on. Erin stared out the window, lost in thought.

Traffic picked up the closer they got to Four Corners. The RV park on the edge of town was full and featured a sign: "Welcome, Needlecrafters."

"Mary Beth said most of the activity was in a park not

far from downtown." Gwendolyn found a parking space with a sign that said it was designated for people attending the needlecraft fair.

They piled out of the car. Across the street was a park filled with tents and booths. One end of the park was for food. Hot dogs, crab cakes, and cotton candy were all advertised with big signs to lure people in. A large number of people were shuffling in and out of the high school next to the park, indicating that there must be more to see inside.

Kate waved at them from across the street where she had found a parking space. The group gathered on the sidewalk, programmed cell numbers into their phones, and split into two groups. Alice and Annie would go with Lily and Taylor, and Gwen and Peggy would see the sights with the two sisters.

"Mary Beth's booth is at the northeast end." Kate pointed in that general direction. "I need to go give her a hand."

"Maybe we can all meet there at, say, three o'clock." Alice adjusted her handbag strap on her shoulder.

The two groups parted. Lily and Taylor walked ahead of the women. But they stayed close enough that Annie could pick up most of their conversation.

"My mom took me to one of these things up in Portland, only it had all kinds of art, painters, and jewelry makers." Lily crossed her arms. Her pink leather purse hung on her forearm.

"You sure do a lot of things with your mom." Taylor slowed her pace and glanced back at Annie and Alice.

"Well, it's just she and I. Daddy works really long hours at the law firm."

"You don't have any brothers and sisters?"

"Mom tried for years to have a baby the normal way, and then she got me."

"You mean you're adopted?"

"Yeah," Lily said.

"Me too," said Taylor.

Lily slowed the pace of her walking. "Are all your brothers and sisters adopted?"

"Two of them are."

"It must get really noisy and messy at your house with all those younger kids."

Taylor shrugged. "It's not too bad. You should come over for a visit."

Lily stopped and turned to face Taylor. "Really?"

"Sure. You can come over anytime."

Warmth pooled in Annie's heart as she watched the two girls draw closer together while they strolled. They paused at a booth where a woman was spinning wool into yarn, and another was dyeing a skein of yarn into a beautiful shade of blue.

Annie crossed her arms. "Now, that's what I call starting from scratch."

The woman at the spinning wheel smiled up at them. "Would you like to spin?"

"I want to try," Taylor sidled into the booth.

Alice took pictures while the spinner instructed Taylor. "Lily, do you want to give it a shot?" Taylor asked.

The petite blond girl pressed her lips together. "I have never done something like that before."

"See, I knew we would find something that you didn't already know how to do." Alice's teasing was lighthearted.

When Lily finished her turn, Alice said, "I want to

try too. Here, Annie, you take my picture."

Annie tried to balance her heavy purse and take the picture. After a moment, she set the purse by her feet.

Alice held up the yarn she had spun, and Annie
snapped the photo. One of the women showed Alice a scarf
knitted from the yarn, and Alice flung it around her neck
and posed dramatically. The girls laughed, and Annie took
a few more pictures. She stepped closer to the booth to
avoid the cluster of people coming toward her.

She angled the camera so that Taylor and Lily could see
the photos, which caused more laughter. A man bumped
into her and apologized. Annie's attention remained focused
on the girls.

Annie handed the camera back to Alice and bent down
to pick up her purse. She turned a half circle. No purse.
Panic tightened her nerves. She scanned the grassy area
behind her.

"What is it?" Alice leaned toward her.

Taylor and Lily had wandered ahead to the next booth.

"My purse, I—" she spotted it leaning against one of the
poles that supported the booth. Annie scooped up the purse
and opened it. Her wallet and keys were still inside, but the
purse had been clasped when she set it down. Now it was open.

Feeling a rising anxiety, Annie studied the crowd milling
past the booths.

Alice placed a hand on Annie's shoulder. "Everything
all right?"

"Nothing seems to be missing, but I …" Annie placed a
palm on her chest where her heart hammered away.

"Did you have the stock certificate in there?"

Annie shook her head. "No, I took it out." But not before she had shown it to half the people in town. Anyone could have seen her taking it out of her purse. Her breath caught in her throat. "You don't think someone was looking for it?"

"Do you need to sit down?"

"I'm not sure." Again, she examined the ever-changing faces of the crowd. It could have been anyone. Whoever it was, he or she must have followed them from Stony Point. They must have been watching her when she was in Stony Point, during the numerous times she had taken the certificate out to show it to people.

"Maybe we just need to get away from this crowd. I noticed a little ice cream shop downtown when we drove in. You can catch your breath," Alice suggested, placing a supportive hand on her friend's shoulder.

Annie clasped her purse shut. "That sounds like a wonderful idea."

Alice and Annie caught up with the girls. They worked their way to the edge of the fair and then crossed the street. Though people wandered on the sidewalk, the crowd thinned quite a bit compared to the booths at the fair. Annie still felt stirred up as they stepped into the ice cream shop.

The shop was decorated to look like a turn-of-a-century ice cream parlor. Lace curtains and framed magazine covers from the era added a nice touch. The sales clerk wore a Gibson-girl dress and black high-button shoes. Annie doubted, however, that the nose ring was period dress. Only a few of the tables were occupied.

The girls got their ice cream cones and found a place at a table. Annie licked her orange sherbet cone. A shiver ran down her spine that had nothing to do with the cold treat. She glanced around at the patrons in the parlor.

Alice took a first lick of her peppermint ice cream cone. Her eyes searched Annie's.

"I don't mean to spoil our good time, but I think I need to go for a walk to calm my nerves," Annie said.

"I understand. I'll hang out with the girls."

Annie stepped outside into the sunshine. Some of the downtown shops were closed, but many had signs that welcomed needlecrafters. She walked past a hardware store and a café filled with diners. Annie rubbed her arm. Was someone following her in an attempt to get the stock certificates?

The smell of the ocean tingled in Annie's nose as she turned a corner. She walked past a darkened doctor's office. Annie stopped short when she came to the next shop. The lettering on the window said, "Ocean Side Partners LLC."

Shading her eyes, she pressed close to the glass and peered inside the dark office. None of the furnishings indicated what kind of business it was. Two desks and two office chairs, a door with lettering on it Annie couldn't discern and several nice bronze sculptures of boats displayed on columnlike pedestals populated the room.

Ocean Side Partners was located in Four Corners. Now she had something to work with. Finding a phone number and calling Ocean Side Partners first thing Monday morning would be a cinch. Annie gazed up and down the street. She was completely alone.

She strode back up to the main street where she found Alice and the girls standing outside the hardware store.

"Better?" Alice asked.

Annie nodded. "And I found Ocean Side Partners."

"No kidding? That's amazing," Alice said.

Annie's phone rang. She lifted it out of her purse. "Hello."

"Mary Beth has just informed us that there is a Ferris wheel down by the lakeshore." Annie recognized Peggy's voice.

"We'll meet you there in five minutes." Annie clicked her phone shut. "Who's up for an amusement park ride?"

They made their way down to the shore. Within minutes, the four older women and the teens were rising up in the air. Annie shared a seat with Erin. Behind her, she could hear Mackenzie and Lily chatting about the things they had seen at the fair.

The chairs eased up to the highest point on the Ferris wheel. The operator stopped the wheel to let more passengers on.

The view of the sound, the rocky shore, and gulls diving gracefully into the gently rolling waves was breathtaking. Annie felt light-headed.

"Do you suppose your grandmother ever cross-stitched anything like the view from up here?" Mackenzie said from behind her.

"I'm sure she would have been inspired by it," shouted Annie. All of the distress she had felt about her purse being rifled through dissipated. Annie breathed in the fresh air. When she looked over at Erin, she was smiling. The Ferris wheel cranked to life, and everyone screamed as the chairs waggled back and forth.

By the time the group decided to head back home, the fair was winding down, and the sun was low on the horizon. Kate had decided to stay and help Mary Beth pack up. She offered the keys to Peggy.

Annie rode in Gwen's car, this time with Taylor and Mackenzie. The talk was much livelier as the girls chatted about their day and asked questions about various needle-craft projects they had seen. Gwen never got around to turning the music on.

It was nearly dark when they returned to A Stitch in Time. The girls had phoned ahead so parents were waiting. The older women waited until the last girl climbed into a car and drove away.

Alice stood beside Annie. "Do you suppose that made a difference in their attitude about the project?"

Annie watched the red taillights of Lily's mom's car disappear. "We'll just have to wait and see."

As Annie drove home, a sense of joy filled her thoughts. The windows in the old Victorian house were dark when she pulled up. She stepped into Grey Gables, clicked on the light, and refilled the food dish for a complaining Boots. She drifted up the stairs feeling lighter than air.

Even thoughts about someone taking her purse couldn't deflate her spirits. Some days were just good that way. The teen girls hadn't totally committed to the project, yet something had changed today in a positive way. She slipped underneath her soft comforter and fell asleep thinking Gram would have loved a day like today.

The next morning, Annie sipped her coffee while standing on the porch enjoying the view of the ocean. When the landline rang, she stepped into the living room and picked up.

"Annie, Ian here. Listen, I've got some news for you about the Joan that left the package in Betsy's attic. Can you join me for breakfast at The Cup & Saucer?"

Annie checked her watch. She had been waiting for the public library to open so she could hunt down the phone number for Ocean Side Partners. There had been a message from Katrina at Seaside that she wanted Annie to come by and meet the women who were interested in the project. "Sure, I have to come into town anyway. See you in ten minutes."

The breakfast rush at The Cup & Saucer was just getting underway when Annie stepped into the restaurant. The scent of cinnamon and maple syrup hung in the air. Ian was sitting at his usual table. Annie didn't see Peggy anywhere. Maybe this was her day off.

Annie settled into a chair opposite Ian, who was all smiles.

The waitress came over and set down menus.

"I don't need to see the menu. I know I want one of your famous cinnamon rolls." The smell of the rolls had already made her mouth water. How could she not have one?

"A woman after my own heart," said Ian, turning his focus to the waitress. "I'll have my usual."

The waitress nodded and gathered up the menus. Ian ate here so much that he had a "usual" for breakfast.

Annie scooted her chair closer in, rested her elbows on the table, and laced her fingers together. "So what did you find out?"

"Like I said, I had it in my head that a woman named Joan visited here for a while sometime around 1997. I kept thinking she was staying with a Stony Point resident."

"She wasn't?"

"I had dinner with the city council last night at the Maplehurst Inn. That's when everything clicked for me."

Annie had been in the Maplehurst Inn, a beautiful co-lonial-style hotel that boasted a fancy dining room. "And?" Annie wiggled in her chair, tensing with anticipation.

"There was a Joan who visited here for over a month, and she stayed at the Maplehurst. The owner remembers her because she stayed so long, and she keeps all her guest books. Joan's last name was Whitlock."

"Oh, Ian, thank you," Annie gushed.

"We couldn't talk for long because the restaurant start-ed to get busy, but she is going to rack her memory and see if she can come up with anything else. You are welcome to swing by and talk to her. Do you have a pen?"

Annie clicked open her purse and handed the pen to Ian. He wrote on a napkin. "This is the owner's name and private phone number; she said you can come by or call anytime."

Annie took the napkin and read Ian's evenly spaced let-tering. "Thanks."

"Anytime." Ian offered her a heartwarming smile.

The waitress brought Ian an egg over easy, whole-wheat toast with strawberry jam, and a glass of water that was half ice with a slice of lemon. Ian smothered his egg with ketchup as Annie dug into her cinnamon roll.

They talked about the sawmill Ian's family owned, and then the conversation turned to the intergenerational project.

"Let's not call a press conference just yet," Annie cau-tioned. "We are still trying to pull everything together." She took a bite of gooey cinnamon roll. The sweetness lingered on her tongue.

"I know you can do it." Ian took a last bite of toast. He checked his watch. "You'll have to excuse me; I've got a meeting in fifteen minutes."

Annie rose to her feet. "I need to get to the library anyway." She stepped out onto Main Street and headed toward the library. She knew Joan's last name. She knew where Ocean Side Partners was. Maybe before the week was over, the stock certificates would be returned to their rightful owner.

Annie entered the library Great Room. Valerie Duffy, the circulation librarian, stood at the Circulation Desk. She looked up and smiled when she saw Annie.

"May I help you with something?" Valerie adjusted her oversized glasses.

"Do you have a phone book for Four Corners?"

"We only keep the books for towns within a hundred miles of Stony Point. We could try the online phone book for Maine."

Valerie led Annie to three computers in the far end of the library. She seated herself in front of a computer and gestured for Annie to take a seat beside her. The librarian typed in the information. No phone number came up for an Ocean Side Partners in Four Corners, Maine.

Annie leaned toward the computer. "Really? I was just there; I saw the office. Does the phone book have white pages too?"

Valerie nodded.

"Can you see if there is a listing for Joan Whitlock or Therese Marie Gilkerson in Four Corners?"

Valerie's fingers tapped the keys. She pushed Enter; then she shook her head. "No one listed by those names in Four Corners. I can widen the search to all of Maine."

A girl of about 6, dressed head to toe in pink, came up

to them. "Can you help me? I want to find a book about Yellowstone Park."

"Sure, sweetie." Valerie excused herself.

Annie stared at the screen that indicated there were "no results" for the name Joan Whitlock. In fact, there were no Whitlocks in the area. A search for all of Maine yielded no results as well. She closed the window on the phone book and went to a main search engine. She typed "Ocean Side Partners LLC." A website came up for an Ocean Side Partners in New Hampshire. Nothing on the website said anything about Four Corners, Maine. From what she could tell, this Ocean Side Partners was in the construction business.

This was perplexing. She hadn't been imagining things. She'd seen the sign on the window in Four Corners. If she had to, she would drive back up there. The office would be open during the week. She quickly wrote down the phone number for the New Hampshire business. The phone call to this Ocean Side Partners would have to wait. She needed to get to her meeting with Katrina at Seaside Hills.

Annie had decided that it was best to be honest with the women by telling them that they didn't have a solid commitment from the teens yet. Even if the teens decided not to be involved, the Hook and Needle Club could make it a two-generation project. As she turned onto Elm Street, she allowed herself just a tiny bit of hope that everything would come together.

Katrina was waiting for her in the foyer. "The ladies are so excited. I've got four women who have shown interest."

Katrina led Annie down the hallway to the dining room where the older women waited.

Annie took a deep breath and entered the dining room.

~ 9 ~

*T*he women sat around a table in the far corner of the unoccupied dining room. Though sounds of water running and pots banging came from the open door of a kitchen, all of the food trays in the dining room were clean and empty. Annie recognized the Joan she had already met, as well as one of the women she had seen knitting that night in the solarium, a small woman with candy-apple–red hair.

Katrina leaned closer to Annie as they approached. "They like working in the dining room because the lighting is better. They come in between meals and have scheduled a standing meeting on Thursday nights. I don't know why we didn't think of it sooner. It took all of them getting to-gether to come up with the idea. This has been good for them already."

Joan glanced up from her knitting, a smile gracing her lips. She whispered to the other women, who all looked in Annie's direction.

Katrina placed a hand on Annie's back. "Ladies, this is Annie Dawson."

"We were pretty sure it was her," said the redheaded knitter. "I'm Estelle. And this is Viola." Estelle indicated the woman next to her, who had started on a crochet project in purple. Viola had short, blond hair cut close to her face. Her jacket and her skirt were made of matching red plaid.

A tall woman, whose half-glasses rested on her beaklike nose, looked up from her needlepoint. "I'm Frieda."

Annie detected a slight twang when Frieda spoke—Oklahoma or Texas maybe.

"When do we get to meet the girls?" Joan's eyes sparkled behind her wire-rimmed glasses.

The heaviness of the hope on the women's faces weighed on Annie. She took in a deep breath. Honesty was always the best approach. "We are still putting things together with the teens."

"They could come here to our work space for our Thursday night meeting." Joan did a Vanna White sweep of the dining room.

Katrina rested a supportive hand above Annie's elbow. "That is a good idea. We could make an evening of it."

Viola smoothed out her plaid skirt. "It sounds like this whole thing is still kind of in the *maybe* stage."

Even though there was no animosity in Viola's observation, Annie felt a jab to her heart. These ladies were all so sweet and so eager. "Some of the girls seem kind of interested, but I don't have clear commitment from all of them. Teenagers are so hard to understand."

All of the women nodded.

Estelle shook her head. "My, my, some things never change. I understand. I raised five children, two girls and three boys."

Joan rose to her feet. "You just let those girls know that they are welcome here, and we will be delighted to work with them."

Annie fiddled with a button on her shirt. "They have

been slow to give me a clear answer, but by Wednesday I will have a definite yes or no." She wished she had better news to share.

Katrina cleared her throat. "Maybe the best use of our time would be for Annie to visit with you ladies for a while. You can talk about what you think your strengths as needle-crafters are and share some of your project ideas."

"That sounds like a wonderful idea." Joan patted her tight, steel-gray curls.

Katrina excused herself. Annie sat in the circle of older women talking about projects past and future. Even with just these four women, there was a rich heritage of skill and creativity. How wonderful it would be to connect them to the next generation. Her resolve grew as she listened and shared. This project was a small thing in a small town, but it mattered in a big way. She knew from having seen her own daughter through the teen years that you can't force an adolescent to do anything. But because the teens had had time to think about it, she hoped they would see the value of the project.

Annie said goodbye to the women, feeling as if she had made four new friends. As she walked down that long hall-way that led to the Seaside entrance, she prayed that every-thing would come together. The idea of disappointing those sweet women would be a lot to bear.

*　*　*　*

Annie drove down the hill toward Main Street. She had just picked up her groceries at Magruder's when she remembered that she needed to call Ocean Side Partners in New Hampshire. She placed her groceries on the passenger seat of her Malibu and slipped in behind the wheel.

Once she was home and the groceries were put away, she dug the phone number out of her purse and called. She paced while she waited for someone to pick up. She filled the kettle with water.

A woman with a clear, high voice answered. "Hello, Ocean Side Partners. How may I help you?"

Annie placed the kettle on the burner and flipped it on high. She hesitated, not sure how to phrase her inquiry. "I … um … I was wondering if you are the same Ocean Side Partners that I saw in Four Corners, Maine?"

"Why yes, we are. We just opened a branch office there. Were you interested in one of our vacation condos that will be going up there soon?" The woman's voice was pleasant and businesslike.

Annie pressed the phone harder against her ear, strategizing the best approach to get the answers she needed. "I couldn't find a phone number for the Four Corners office anywhere."

"That office is so new. I doubt they are even listed. We're just doing the update on the website this week." Suspicion colored the woman's words. "Is there something I could help you with?"

Annie opened the cupboard where she kept the tea. Carrying on a charade gnawed at her conscience. She didn't want to waste the woman's time or be dishonest. "Here is the thing. I found some stock certificates from Ocean Side Partners that were issued in 1997. I assume if you are expanding, the stock is doing well?"

"Are you the holder of the stock?"

She understood the woman's reluctance to give out information. She was just trying to protect the investors. "I found the stock certificates in my grandmother's attic, and I want to return them to their rightful owner, but I am having trouble locating her."

"Oh ... I see." There was a slight pause as though the woman had transferred the phone from one ear to the other. "Well, whoever purchased that stock in 1997 got in on the ground floor. They have at least tripled in value."

Annie's throat constricted. The stock was worth a substantial sum. That made it more important than ever to get the certificates back to their owner. "I don't suppose you would have a record with addresses and phone numbers of stock purchasers? I think Joan Whitlock bought the stock for someone named Therese Marie Gilkerson."

"So you are saying the purchaser and the person the stock is registered to might be two different people?"

Annie wrinkled her forehead. "I guess that is what I am saying."

"We would have a record of each stock number and the registered holder. If a transfer took place, we would only have the registered holder, not the original purchaser." A pause filled the phone line. "I would really like to help you. It sounds like you are trying to do a good thing, but that information is confidential. I can't give it out over the phone."

Annie leaned back against the counter as a sense of defeat spread through her. "I understand, but I just want to return the stock certificates. What if this Therese person doesn't even know about them?" If Therese had never gotten the gift of the physical certificates, maybe Joan hadn't ever transferred the registration.

"It does seem like she would have come forward by now if she knew about the stock's value." The woman spoke slowly as though she were problem solving.

And where was Joan in all this? Something had kept her from coming back for the certificates. Annie thanked the woman and hung up, more perplexed than ever. She was about to close the cupboard door when she noticed the mouse droppings. A quick investigation revealed that her granola bars had been nibbled on.

Annie let out a heavy sigh. "Guess who has moved downstairs?" Wiping her frustration with the mouse from her mind, she leaned against the counter. A thought she hadn't previously considered popped into her head. Therese might not have come looking for the certificates because she didn't know they had been intended for her, but what if Joan was dead? Maybe that was why she hadn't come back for the stock certificates. A chill ran down Annie's back.

The whistling of the kettle jerked her out of her musing. Annie poured the hot water into a teacup and swished the bag back and forth. Anxiety churned in her stomach. Everything was so unsettled and so uncertain. She didn't know if she would be able to pull the intergenerational project together, and she didn't know if she ever would be able to return those certificates. She gritted her teeth. The final straw was that silly mouse.

She remembered something Gram always used to say: "God has a way of working these things out."

She brought the steaming cup of tea up to her face, allowing the minty scent to relax her. At least tomorrow she had the Hook and Needle Club meeting. The ladies would know what to do.

* * * *

On Tuesday, Annie rose early, feeling rejuvenated by a good night's sleep. She spent some time staining the boards Wally had brought in for the new shelving in the library. Then she cleaned up and dressed for the meeting. She'd finished the yellow infant hat and jacket, and had decided to do another set in lilac. Mary Beth would have the yarn she needed.

She arrived fifteen minutes early and was looking over Mary Beth's selection of yarn when Stella and Peggy showed up together. While Kate rang up her purchases, Gwen and Alice sauntered in.

Gwen held up some light gray yarn. "I was so inspired by what I saw at that needlecraft fair that I decided to go all primitive and spin my own wool."

"You made that from raw wool?" Alice gathered it into her hands.

Gwen shrugged. "It's a little rough, I know, but I had fun."

"I got a few ideas of my own wandering around that place," Alice added with her usual exuberance. "Do you think the girls were inspired?"

The three of them wandered over to where Peggy and Stella had already found chairs next to each other. Kate and

Mary Beth were still busy with customers.

"It's so hard to tell with teenagers." Gwen settled into her usual chair.

"I think it did make a difference." Annie said, placing her tote beside her chair. "I'm just hoping it was enough for the girls to be willing to do the project with the Seaside residents."

Peggy fidgeted on her chair. "I know I had fun on the trip."

Mary Beth, who had been listening to the women talk while she stood outside the circle of chairs, commented, "The indifference and the feet dragging can be a trial, but just remember: when it comes to a teenager, sometimes that is all for show. They might just be dying to be a part of this."

"Tomorrow is the final day. We need a clear commitment from them." Rising anxiety pinched at the back of Annie's neck.

Gwen cleared her throat. "Can I be honest with you ladies?"

The other women nodded. Peggy scooted forward and leaned toward Gwen.

Gwen rested her hands in her lap and took in a breath. "I have a hard time with Lily. She acts like she knows everything. It's just … difficult to relate to her."

"Maybe she is just not the girl you should focus on," Annie suggested.

"She makes me bristle a little bit too." Alice shifted in her chair. "Since Mackenzie has shown an interest in cross-stitch, I feel like I can build a relationship with her."

Mary Beth combed her fingers through her graying hair.

"All the girls are very different. Taylor seems able to connect with anyone."

Annie pulled some of the purple yarn out of the skein, enjoying the soft feel in her hand. "I think once Erin gains some confidence, she'll come out of her shell. She's a really sweet girl." The problem was she had no idea how to build that confidence.

"It just seems there must be something we can do for Lily," Peggy tugged on the collar of her pink uniform. "I know I can't be there that much." She flashed her silver fingernails at everyone. "I should take her to my sister, and then we could bond over getting our nails done."

"Maybe there is nothing we can do. Some people are just that way." Gwen pulled her glasses out of the case and placed them on her face. "No matter what you do, they don't change."

Stella let out a huff that she intended for everyone to hear. "All this talk about the trip and the teens." Her knitting needles clicked. "Maybe I should come to the meeting and straighten this Lily girl out. You are doing knitting for your lesson tomorrow, aren't you?"

The room fell silent for a moment.

"We'd love to have you." Alice threaded a needle while her cross-stitch lay on her lap.

Mary Beth offered Annie a furtive glance. Mary Beth's face was etched with concern. They were probably thinking the same thing. They had wanted to include Stella, but was "straightening out" what Lily really needed?

"Have you had any progress on getting those stock certificates back to their owner since you found Ocean Side

Partners?" Alice flipped open a pattern book she had brought with her.

Annie was glad the conversation had turned to the stock certificates. "I did find out that the certificates have increased a lot in value. But I am no closer to finding Joan or Therese."

Alice picked up her cross-stitch, tightened her hoop, and poked her needle through the aida cloth. "You don't have any leads at all?"

"Just one. Ian found out that a woman named Joan had stayed at Maplehurst Inn. He thought the inn's owner might have some insight. He gave me the owner's name. Linda somebody."

Alice perked up. "Oh, I love the Maplehurst Inn. They lay out the nicest Friday brunches."

Gwen said, "We should all go. Make a morning of it?"

"I don't know, ladies, we are starting to set a pattern. We're becoming the club that meets two days a week instead of one," Annie teased as she felt the lively banter improve her mood.

"I don't see how that could be a bad thing." Alice elbowed Annie.

"I am fond of the Maplehurst brunches." Stella's eyes sparkled. "They have the best quiche in town."

Peggy rose to her feet and stretched. "I'm afraid I have to work."

"Me too," said Mary Beth. "Kate will be in the shop as well."

"The four of us can go anyway," Gwen suggested. The women agreed to meet at the inn at ten o'clock on Friday.

The talk turned to the quartet from Portland that Stella had snagged to play at the Cultural Center, and Annie focused on her crocheting. She was glad to see Stella show an interest in participating with the rest of the club on outings, but uneasiness about tomorrow's teen meeting plagued her. Though Stella had never had any children of her own, she had all kinds of ideas of how children should be raised. Maybe Lily's know-it-all attitude hid some deep wound. Would Stella be sensitive to that?

Annie worked out her anxiety with her crocheting. Her hook grabbed the yarn and formed the rows of stitches easily. As usual, the hour flew by.

Thoughts about Joan played at the corner of her mind. Annie stopped crocheting.

"You've got that look on your face," Alice said as she leaned close to her friend, eyebrows drawn together.

"What look?"

"The *I'm worried* look."

The other women got up from their chairs as the meeting broke up. They wandered around the store, still visiting with each other.

Annie pulled taut the yarn in her hand and then wound it around her finger. "I was just thinking. Someone broke into my house. We know now that the stock certificates are worth something."

Alice put her cross-stitch back in her bag and zipped it up. "I see what you are saying." She rose to her feet. "You are wondering—if the stock was so valuable, why wouldn't Joan come back for it after all these years?"

Annie tensed. "I am starting to think that maybe the

reason Joan didn't come back to Gram's house was because she *couldn't* come back."

"You mean—" Alice's face blanched. "You can't let your mind go there. We don't know anything for sure."

"I'm just not sure what we are dealing with here anymore," Annie whispered.

— 10 —

Wednesday afternoon as she got ready for the teen meeting, Annie felt a mixture of excitement and anxiety. By five o'clock, she would know if they could go forward with the intergenerational project. As she looked in the bedroom mirror and ran a brush through her hair, she told herself that it didn't matter. The Hook and Needle Club could keep helping with the class without the project, and maybe they could also step in and do something with the Seaside ladies. Even though she tried to convince herself she'd be OK if the girls weren't on board with the project, her churning stomach told her their participation mattered to her.

Annie went down to the kitchen. Boots twirled around her legs as Annie poured herself a glass of milk before leaving. She'd found more evidence that the mice had migrated. One of her plastic storage containers had some telltale teeth marks on it. Annie narrowed her eyes at the cat. "Why aren't you doing your job?" She knew the gray feline was capable of hunting. When the weather was nice, she would go outside and leave little "gifts" for Annie on the porch. "The indoor mice just aren't interesting to you, huh?"

Boots meowed a response.

Annie finished up her milk and went into town. Though she had intended to be early, Erin and Mackenzie along with Stella and Gwen were already picking out yarn and needles for their next lesson. Lily and Taylor were seated and working on their projects. No doubt Lily had purchased the yarn days in advance.

Erin stood in front of a wall of yarn separated into wooden boxes by color. The girl was so deeply in thought that a crease appeared between her eyebrows. She held up a pair of knitting needles. "Mary Beth said these were the best size for a beginner to start with." She turned back toward the wall of yarn. "I just can't decide on what color of yarn I want."

"The first time I saw you in class you were wearing a pair of pink high-tops. I liked seeing a little pop of color on you."

Erin lifted her head. "You noticed that about me?"

"Of course I did. I notice a lot about you."

Erin shot a glance toward her sister and then stared at the floor, twisting her foot inward. "Sometimes I feel a little invisible."

Annie lifted Erin's chin and brushed a strand of hair behind her ear. "You're not invisible to me."

Erin's expression warmed. "Thanks," she whispered. She turned back toward the wall of yarn. "I still don't know what color to pick."

Annie grabbed a skein of fuchsia yarn and placed it in Erin's hand. "You could make a nice scarf out of that to match your high-tops."

Erin brushed her hand over the yarn. "If I could ever finish anything …"

"I know these projects have been a struggle for you, but you'll find something you like, and you'll just take off with it."

Erin shrugged. "Knitting is the last lesson." Sadness colored her words. "I wouldn't count on me taking off today."

Annie's heart ached for Erin. "Maybe needlecraft isn't your thing. Sooner or later, you'll discover what you are good at."

"I don't know about that. Mackenzie is the one who is good at everything." Erin stood up a little straighter and looked directly at Annie. "I sure have liked coming to the class though. And the trip was fun too."

"We've loved having you." Annie gave Erin a sideways hug, squeezing her shoulder. Erin had such a pure, sweet heart. Something just had to click for this kid.

"Erin, hurry up." Mackenzie stood at the register while Kate rang up the purchases.

The doorbell dinged and Vanessa, Kate's daughter, stepped across the threshold. Kate's face brightened. "You came."

Vanessa wore shorts and flip-flops, not exactly spring attire. She raised her hands up, palms outward. "My mother would not stop talking about what a fun trip you guys had. She made me feel like I was missing out on a good time. So here I am. I already have needles and yarn."

"We are always glad to have you," Mary Beth said.

"Hey, I know you." Vanessa took her needles out of her bag and ambled toward Mackenzie. "You sit behind me in algebra."

Mackenzie clearly recognized her. "So is Mr. Simpson an alien or what?"

"Do you mean the big ears and bug eyes, or the way he is oddly excited about finding the value of x?"

Both girls laughed. Mackenzie and Vanessa made their way to the circle of chairs at the front of the store.

Everyone settled into a chair. Gwen sat at the front of the class, knitting needles poised for instruction. "Everyone, this is Stella. She is our other knitter."

Stella had found a seat beside Lily. The older woman looked more ready for the opera than a knitting lesson in her brocade jacket, up-do hairstyle, and diamond earrings.

Gwen cleared her throat and explained to the girls how to cast on. "Stella, you can jump in at any time."

Lily lifted her chin, keeping her mouth tight. "I already know how to do this."

Turning toward Lily, Stella stiffened a little and raised her eyebrows but didn't say anything.

Annie took a seat beside Erin. There hadn't been time to discuss the Seaside project right away. It would just have to wait until the end of class.

Stella leaned close to Lily. "Oh dear, I think you've dropped a stitch."

"No, I didn't," Lily blurted. "My mom taught me how to do this. I know what I am doing."

Annie tensed, preparing for Stella's *straightening out.*

The older woman's lips pursed. "Your mom taught you how to knit. What a wonderful gift. My mother died when I was little." A gentle quality permeated Stella's voice.

The movement of Lily's fingers slowed. "I guess it is a neat thing."

"You really are doing a nice job." Stella examined the six inches of knitting Lily had completed, stretching it out in her hand so she could look at it closer.

Lily examined her work. "I guess maybe I did drop a stitch here."

"It would be nothing to go back and start over from that point. You completed your rows pretty quickly, and they are so perfect."

Lily lifted her head and held her work out at arm's length. "Probably, I could do that. I could fix it."

"I know you could," Stella encouraged.

Lily turned sideways to look at Stella, and an expression of warmth passed between them.

"Yes, I can." Lily unraveled a row with the softest of smiles on her face.

Mackenzie held up her two rows of knitting. "I'm really slow at this. It could take me like a million years."

Vanessa leaned close to her friend and whispered something that made her laugh. Erin watched the two girls and then wiggled in her seat before she hung her head.

"Usually your sister sits beside you." Annie leaned toward Erin, speaking in a low voice.

The two older girls continued to giggle, heads bent close together, cupping their hands over their mouths and whispering.

"Not today, though." Erin stared at the floor.

"I'm just not getting this." Taylor held up her tangled mess. Her stitches were all different sizes.

"Why don't you come sit beside me?" Gwen suggested. "I'll walk you through it." She looked at the work Taylor had done. "You're probably going to have to unravel all of that."

Taylor laughed. "That bad, huh?"

"I like the way you can laugh at your mistakes," Gwen said.

"Win some, lose some," Taylor said with a shrug. "Can't be good at everything." She undid the knitting she had started. "So, ladies, what's the scoop on the project with the old people?"

Annie's breath caught. She chose her words carefully. "Four women at Seaside are interested. I was just waiting for all of you to tell me yes or no. Either we can make arrangements for all of you to get together, or we can forget the whole thing."

"You know I'm in." Taylor continued to pull out her knitting. "I thought it was a great idea from the start."

"I'll do it if Vanessa does it," said Mackenzie, hugging the arm of her new friend.

A puzzled look crossed Vanessa's face. "Does what?"

"Annie wants us to make some stuff for the new babies at Stony Point Hospital," Mackenzie explained. "I can't remember what it is called. A bassinet, I think."

"A layette." Gwen seemed amused by Mackenzie's explanation.

"We would work with the residents at Seaside. They know way more than we do about this kind of stuff." Taylor grimaced at the spider's web of yarn she had created. "I think it would be neat, but I doubt I'll be knitting anything."

Erin said, "I'd like to do it." She shrugged. "I don't know how much help I would be. The older ladies would probably have to do most of the work. But I would like to help."

Lily's shoulders stiffened. "I still say old people—" Her eyes darted to the side where Stella sat with her hands folded in her lap. "It might be an OK thing to do."

"That settles it then." Annie tried not to gush, but inside

she was dancing like Snoopy. "All five of you are in." *Yes, yes, yes, this is all going to come together.*

Alice's expression took on a glow as well. "So when will the girls be able to meet with the Seaside women?"

"The ladies at Seaside have a regular meeting on Thursday evenings at seven o'clock after dinner, and they are open to having you come," Annie said. "I know it's kind of short notice. Can everyone make that time?"

All of the girls but Lily nodded.

"I'll have to ask my mother," Lily quipped.

Annie turned her head to hide the laugh that threatened to escape. Lily always had to put up some protest. That was just who she was. The kid grew on you. All of them did.

The rest of the meeting passed quickly. Erin and Taylor never got very far past their home row of knitting. Annie basked in positive feelings as parents came to pick up teens.

Mary Beth rested a hand on Annie's shoulder. "You are doing a good thing here."

After gathering her things, Stella bustled toward the door.

"Thanks for coming today," Annie said, "and for working with Lily."

Stella squared her shoulders. "The way you talked about her, I thought I was going to meet a brat. She is a sweet girl. Those cute little tight braids. Reminds me of myself when I was her age."

Annie had a feeling it wasn't just the braids that reminded Stella of herself at that age. "We'll see you Thursday evening," Annie said as Stella went out the door. She watched from the window as Stella's driver, Jason, opened the door of the Lincoln Continental for her.

Alice hugged her friend from behind. "What are you thinking?"

"This meeting went so well, I am dreading going home. Every time I think about that mouse, it upsets me. Wally has the library all torn to pieces, and now he has another job that is tying him up. Home doesn't feel like home."

"Construction always goes like that, doesn't it?" Alice was empathetic.

Annie said, "That library is going to look great when it is all spiffed up, but living in a construction zone makes me crazy."

"I don't have any parties tonight. What say we grab a bite to eat at The Cup & Saucer, and then I will help you look for the mouse?"

"Or mice. I'm not sure how many I am dealing with. Dinner out sounds like a good idea."

After a blue-plate special of spaghetti and meatballs, Annie and Alice headed back to Grey Gables. Rain spattered lightly against the windshield as Annie drove toward the old house. She sighed when the house came into view. A lot of work still needed to be done on the outside of Gram's place. She'd taken on the library job because she'd thought it would be a small one.

Annie fumbled with her keys. "Shall I make a pot of tea? Vanilla almond for you, right?"

Alice laughed as they stepped inside. "What does one serve at a mouse hunt?"

"We would have to consult the etiquette books on that." Once in the kitchen, Annie set her purse on the corner of the counter and filled the kettle.

Alice placed her hand on her hips. "OK, where do you think they might be?"

"I've set traps under the sink and where they nibbled on my granola bars, and I didn't have any takers." Annie ran her fingers through her hair. "You don't think they would still stay upstairs but come downstairs to eat, do you?"

Alice shrugged. "Could be. I don't have any friends who are mice. You can't find any holes where they might be getting in?"

"Not in the attic or the kitchen." She laid out the teacups.

Alice started opening and closing cupboards calling, "Here mousy mousy."

"Now I see how this works." Annie laughed.

Boots trotted into the kitchen and meowed at Alice.

Alice scrunched up her face at the cat. "That's a pretty big mouse."

Annie laughed even harder, patting her palm on her chest. "Thank you, I needed a good laugh." Still trying to catch her breath, she poured the hot water in the teapot.

"Class went well today. I guess I just need to focus on that—on the things that are going well, not on the things that are frustrating me."

"I find myself looking forward to that class almost as much as the Hook and Needle Club. Those girls have filled a hole in my life I didn't even know was there." Just a hint of sadness entered Alice's voice.

"Life has a way of coming full circle like that."

"I always wanted children, but John was never open to

the idea." Alice sipped her tea and let out an *ah-h-h* sound. "Such is life, huh?"

Though Alice tried to hide her sorrow with a quick smile, Annie could see the depth of pain there. "Being with the girls has been a good thing for all of us."

Alice nodded. "Now, about your mouse. I suppose we can tear the attic apart looking for the mouse house. If they won't come to the traps, you're just going to have to figure out where they are living." Alice placed a hand on her hip and scrunched up her face.

Annie groaned. "I don't want to think about it anymore. This house is so big. They could be anywhere." She sat on one of the counter stools. "I'm tired of the case of the missing mouse house."

"Are you getting tired of Grey Gables, maybe contemplating going back to Texas?" Alice's voice had a lilt to it.

"Oh no, it's nothing like that." Annie turned slightly on her stool, taking in the whole of the kitchen and all of the improvements she had made so far. "It's just that I have this memory of how this place was when I was a kid and used to visit Gram. I think I am trying too hard to recapture that feeling. Or maybe it is just that I didn't see the peeling paint and scratched floors when I was ten."

"Betsy filled this place with love. She truly practiced hospitality. That probably covered up a lot of the flaws." Alice crossed her arms over her body. "Or it could be about perspective."

"Perspective?"

"When I was in second grade, everything in Mrs. Stillion's classroom seemed huge. I thought Mrs. Stillion was so glamorous. Years later, I went back to see her, because she was my favorite teacher. When I walked into the classroom and saw those little desks, I felt like a giant. Mrs. Stillion was a pretty lady but not a movie star. The classroom wasn't as bright and colorful as I remembered."

"I suppose you're right. I am remembering the Grey Gables of my childhood through a soft-focus lens." Annie hopped off her stool. "Still, it would be nice to recapture some of the hominess I remember."

"What you are doing will honor Betsy, but you will also put your own mark on Grey Gables."

Annie looked at her insightful friend. "I never thought of it that way, but you're right. I have to make Grey Gables my own, not keep looking in on the past. Once the wiring and the outlets are updated in the library, I'll be able to upgrade my computer and get a printer, something Gram would never have understood."

Alice set her empty teacup on the counter. "Why don't you show me what you have done in the library? Maybe there is something we can do together to hurry the project along."

Annie moved toward the hallway. "You know I'm not good with power tools."

"I might be able to help. I've had to learn a thing or two since my divorce."

Annie entered the library. The shelves on one wall had all been taken down. Wally and Douglas had repaired part of the wall they had torn out to update the wiring and add outlets. Gram's favorite chair and Grandpa's oak desk had been pushed to the middle of the room and covered with sheets. Annie sighed and tried to picture the day when this would once again be the cozy place she remembered.

"What are all those boxes?"

"The books I took off the shelves." Annie bent over and flipped open one of the cardboard boxes. "Gram has some really wonderful books." She held up a volume. "Lots of stuff that is out of print. I read so many of these books when I was a kid. I can't bring myself to get rid of anything."

"There must be something you can part with to create a little more space." Alice kneeled beside her on the floor. She lifted a stack of magazines out of another box. "Why was she saving these?" Alice held up several women's magazines. The covers were faded and the model's hairstyles indicated they were from the 1980s.

"OK, those can probably be thrown out." Annie picked up a magazine with a dog on the cover called *Veterinarian Times*. "This was probably Grandpa's. It can go." She grabbed another magazine. *New England Needlecraft Arts*. She flipped through the magazine. "I assume she saved this because her work was in it. It might be a keeper." She turned to the table of contents, still not finding any reference to Betsy Holden. But the editor's letter caught her eye. All of the air left her lungs. "Oh my."

Alice leaned closer so she was reading over Annie's shoulder. "Joan Whitlock was the editor of *New England Needlecraft Arts*."

Her mind racing, Annie flipped the page. "The main office was in New Hampshire. That's where the original Ocean Side Partners was. Joan must have lived there." She closed the magazine and stared at the cover of a pretty redheaded woman modeling a crocheted cardigan. "Gram probably had a professional relationship with her. Joan was visiting here, and she got in touch with Gram."

"It's a missing piece to the puzzle," Alice said.

Annie held the magazine to her chest. "Joan must have come here for some other reason. If she had come to see Gram, for sure, Gram would have invited her to stay at Grey Gables."

"Maybe if we can figure out the reason, we can find Joan. If we found Joan, don't you think she would be in touch with this Therese Marie?" Alice's shoulders slumped. "Or are you still thinking something happened to Joan?"

"I don't know, Alice. I really don't know." She looked at the magazine again. "I wonder if this is still being published. My laptop is about to die."

Alice got to her feet. "I can check on my laptop. I need to get home anyway."

Still holding the magazine, Annie said goodbye to Alice and then wandered back into the kitchen. She put away the tea and cookies, and then wiped down the counters. She was shuffling through the mail when the phone rang.

"Hello."

"*New England Needlecraft Arts* went out of business in 1998," Alice informed her.

A shroud of disappointment covered Annie. "Oh well, at least we know what Joan's connection to Gram was." She opened the magazine again, staring at the page that listed the editors and contributing writers. "Do you suppose any of these people who worked with Joan are still around?"

"Maybe."

Annie closed the magazine. "It could just be a wild-goose chase too. You have a good night, my friend." She hung up the phone.

A second later the phone rang again. Alice probably remembered something. Annie picked up the receiver. "Yes, my dear."

A raspy voice came across the line. "You have something I want. Give it back."

Annie's arm went limp as she let the phone fall.

11

*I*cy tendrils crept down Annie's back. She braced her hand on the counter. Her vision blurred as her mind replayed the words of the caller. The voice had cut straight through her. Finally, she let out the breath she had been holding and leaned down to pick up the phone. Caller I.D. said the number was unknown.

Her hands were shaking as she dialed the police station.

"Stony Point Police Station." She recognized Chief Edwards' voice.

"Hello ... I'm ..."

"Mrs. Dawson? Are you all right?"

"I'm ... ah ... I'm ... I just received a threatening phone call."

"Are you in any danger now?"

"I don't think—" The front door. She hadn't locked it after Alice left. "I don't think I am."

With the phone still in her hand, she paced down the hallway to the front door. After locking it, Annie drew back the curtain and stared out onto the dark street.

"Are you still there?"

"Yes, I am still here," Annie's voice cracked.

"Annie, would you like me to send my deputy over?" The chief spoke with professional calm.

"Well, I—" Annie tugged at a strand of hair. She couldn't think straight.

"I'm sending Officer Peters over. Hang in there. He'll be there shortly."

"Thank you." Annie said a prayer of thanks that the chief could be decisive when she could barely put two thoughts together. She hung up and gazed out the window.

Something moved by the bushes. Her heartbeat sped up. Annie blinked. Maybe it was just the wind. She stepped away from the window. The house seemed colder.

Still gripping the phone, Annie sat in the living room, waiting for the officer; her feet planted firmly on the floor, she stared straight ahead. The ticking clock dominated the room. At a time like this, her longing for Wayne grew even stronger. Wayne would speak his calming words and take on that protective attitude he had, and she would find the strength to handle something like this. But Wayne wasn't here. She'd have to find the strength on her own. Annie took in several deep breaths and prayed for her fear to subside.

Whoever wanted these stock certificates had been bold enough to break into her house and now to make that threatening phone call. The culprit had known that one of the stock certificates was in her purse. She was being watched. What was keeping Joan or Therese from coming forward if either of them was the one breaking in and making calls? Maybe there had been something illegal connected with the stock that would surface if one of them came out in the open to claim them.

Maybe this. Maybe that. She was tired of this whole thing. Her heart hadn't stopped racing.

Annie rose to her feet, still rattled by the phone call.

She wanted to hear her daughter's voice. She paced into the hallway while she dialed LeeAnn's number.

"Hello, Sorensen residence. Who do you wish to speak to?" Joanna's little-girl voice caused Annie's heart to swell with affection. LeeAnn must have been working with the twins on phone etiquette.

"Hi, sweetie."

"Grandma," came the gleeful reply.

"How's my best girl?" Annie strolled back into the kitchen.

"Good. We went swimming today, and I jumped in the deep end."

"Good for you." A calm washed over Annie. Just hearing that sweet childish voice made all of the difference in the world. "Grandma sure loves you."

"Love you too, Grandma. You want to talk to Mama?"

"Sure," Annie said.

Annie heard Joanna trotting through the house calling for her mother; her voice grew farther away. A moment later, LeeAnn was on the line.

"Mom, hi, you're calling kind of late. Is everything all right?"

She didn't want to worry LeeAnn. That wasn't why she had called. "Yes, I'm fine. I just was missing you, and I wanted to hear your voice. What have you and the kids been up to?"

LeeAnn filled Annie in on swimming lessons and art projects. Annie told LeeAnn about the intergenerational project. As she listened to the sound of her daughter's voice, tears rimmed in her eyes. She missed them. This was all so much to deal with alone. The thought of going back to Texas seemed very appealing right now.

"All of that sounds so wonderful. I wish I could be there for it," Annie said.

"You know, Mom, you can."

"Yes, I know." She loved Stony Point, but she had her moments of doubt. And this was one of them. She was seriously thinking about going back to Texas.

The doorbell rang.

"LeeAnn, I've got to go." Hearing her daughter's voice had helped her regain a sense of peace.

Annie paced through the house, checking first through the window to make sure it was a police officer outside. She unlocked the door. She recognized the young man in front of her. Officer Cal Peters had been brought in when the previous deputy resigned. He must have decided to stay on permanently. His buzz-cut red hair stood straight up. He couldn't have been a day over twenty. The freckles only added to the effect that he was barely an adult.

Deputy Peters acknowledged Annie with a nod. "Mrs. Dawson. I understand you had a threatening phone call."

"Yes, come in. I'm not sure what we can do. I checked the caller I.D. No number shows up."

The officer stepped into the foyer. "Can you describe the voice for me? Was it a man or a woman?"

Annie searched her memory. She'd been so shocked by the call. "I'm not sure. It could have been either one. The voice was low and raspy."

The officer rested his hands on his belt that held numerous gadgets. "Did it sound like the caller was trying to disguise his or her voice?"

Annie nodded. "That could be. The voice didn't sound

natural. It sounded ... scary."

The officer took out a notebook. "What exactly did the caller say to you?"

"I don't remember the exact words. The voice said something like, 'You have something of mine. I want it back.'" She shivered involuntarily.

"What do you suppose the call was about?"

Annie explained about the stock certificates and then said, "I suppose the call was meant to scare me. To let me know I was being watched. They aren't demanding anything or setting up a time and place for me to return the certificates." In the back of her mind, she wondered if the call wasn't a set-up for the threats to escalate, to make her frightened enough to give over the certificates without questions.

"You think this has something to do with the break in you reported earlier?"

"I think it is all connected to those stock certificates." Annie tried to recall what the voice sounded like.

The officer studied her for a moment. "The chief wanted you to know that he is paying close attention to this."

"I know there isn't a lot for him to go on." The phantom break-in where nothing was taken could probably be written off as her imagining things. And now, all they had to go on with the phone call was her foggy memory of it.

Annie thanked the officer. She drew her sweater around her and watched from the window as the officer got into his car and drove away. She double-checked to make sure all of the doors were locked before heading upstairs. Boots stayed close to her while she got ready for bed.

Annie slipped underneath her comforter. Boots jumped

up on the bed and kneaded the comforter with her paws. Annie drew her covers up to her shoulders.

She missed LeeAnn and the twins, but she wasn't alone here. She felt the comforting support of the Hook and Needle Club ladies. Ian was a friend too. Though thoughts of her friends gave her some peace, Annie feared she was facing a sleepless night alone with Boots in this big old house. When Boots settled down at her feet, Annie listened to her purr until one of them fell asleep.

*   *   *   *

The next day, Annie spent most of her morning preparing the garden plot for planting. It was late afternoon when she checked her watch. She needed to go into town and get ready for the big night of the teens and seniors meeting together for the first time.

After a quick shower, Annie went into the kitchen to prepare a box dinner to eat in town. She wouldn't have time to come back to the house, and she'd been eating a lot of meals out. Though she tried to focus on the get-together at Seaside, her stomach clenched when she thought about the phone call and everything else that had happened.

As she tidied up the kitchen, *The New England Needlecraft Arts* magazine caught her eye where it sat on the corner of the counter. She flipped it to the page that listed the staff members. Her finger trailed down the page until she landed on the name Shelley Holms.

It wouldn't hurt to try to find some of these people. She called information, asking for Keene, New Hampshire, and then requested Shelley's number, bracing herself to hear that there was no listing. The line transferred her to an electronic voice that read the number. Annie grabbed a pen.

After hanging up, she inhaled and dialed the number.

A male voice greeted her.

"Hello, I'm looking for Shelley Holms."

"I'll go get her."

Annie's heart hammered as she tapped the pen on the counter.

"Hello."

"Hi, I'm trying to track down someone who used to work at the *New England Needlecraft Arts* magazine."

"Wow, that was years ago. I was fresh out of college. My first editorial job."

Hope fluttered through Annie. Finally, a lead that wasn't a dead end. "Do you remember a Joan Whitlock?"

"Sure, I remember Joan."

"I know the magazine isn't being published anymore, but do you know what happened to Joan? Are you in touch with her by any chance?"

"After the magazine folded, I really didn't keep in contact with people."

"Do you have any idea how I might get hold of Joan?"

There was a long pause on the line. "Why do you want to find her?" Suspicion had crept into Shelley's voice.

Why would Shelley feel protective of Joan? Annie explained about the stock certificates, and her assumption that Joan Whitlock was the Joan she was looking for.

"Oh." The tension had left Shelley's voice. "Joan and I weren't really close or anything. She never shared personal stuff with me. I can tell you one thing that happened that was kind of weird."

"Yes?" Annie felt the familiar prickling at the back of her neck as she anticipated the answer.

"I was an intern, so I handled reception and correspondence quite a bit." The voice paused on the other end of the line. "I don't know if I should say this. Really, these were just my observations."

"Please, it's important that I find her." Annie tensed. She was so close to getting something solid. She didn't want it to slip out of her fingers. "Any information you have might be helpful."

"OK, I'll tell you. It really looked to me like Joan was trying to wipe out her identity. She got rid of her credit cards and closed out a bank account. She didn't have a home phone number, just a cell. She was paying for almost everything in cash." Shelley blurted out the information without stopping to take a breath.

The chill Annie had felt earlier returned. "Thank you, Shelley."

"Like I said, it was just what I observed."

Annie hung up the phone as thoughts buzzed through her head. What was Joan planning to do if she was getting rid of the paper trail that could identify her? Was she running from something, or had she done something that made her feel she needed to disappear?

Annie grabbed a light floral-print jacket and got in her car. Her head was still in a fog as she drove downtown. She had planned on spending the day in town getting things together for the first meeting between the teens and the seniors tonight. She needed to pick up pattern books and yarn samples from Mary Beth and then help Katrina get the dining room ready, as well as talk about some ice-breaker games to help everyone feel comfortable.

She found a parking place a block from A Stitch in Time. As she made her way up the sidewalk, Annie wondered if her theory that Joan had been involved in something illegal was true. It would explain why she hadn't come back for the stock certificates. What if it had been Joan who had made the cryptic phone call? But what kind of illegal activity would an editor of a needlecraft magazine be involved in? Her grandmother had always been a perceptive person and a good judge of character. She just couldn't picture Gram agreeing to take the stock certificates for safekeeping if Joan was up to something.

Or maybe Joan was a victim. What if she was so afraid of something or someone that she felt she had to disappear?

"Penny for your thoughts." Ian had just stepped out of The Cup & Saucer. Really, the restaurant seemed like Ian's second home. He offered Annie a bright smile.

Annie explained about the threatening phone call and everything that had been spinning through her head. Ian listened sympathetically. Annie'd been so lost in thought, she hadn't even noticed what a sunny, beautiful day it was. Although it was late in the day, the temperature had to be in the 50s. Standing close to Ian with the sun warming her face was a nice reality check. So much in her life was good and right. All of the trouble with the stock certificates tended to block that out.

"This is becoming very serious." Ian squeezed Annie's

arm above the elbow. "You be careful, Annie."

"I will be. I'm just a little spooked."

Just having Ian close made her feel safer. Nothing was going to happen in broad daylight, but she couldn't shake the feeling that someone was keeping tabs on her.

"I've got to get back to the office," Ian said.

"Thank you, Ian, for getting me over a bumpy spot." Annie shaded her eyes from the afternoon sun.

Ian tipped his imaginary hat to her and turned, hands in his pockets. She watched as he ambled down the lamppost-lined street with that easy stride of his. The sun shone on his hair, bringing out the soft highlights. When he turned back around and waved at her, his smile warmed her even more than the sun.

Annie swung by A Stitch in Time to get the supplies from Mary Beth. "I'm so sorry I can't be there tonight," said Mary Beth as she opened a box of yarn that had just been shipped. "This really is your baby, Annie. You have done a great job of making it come together."

"I couldn't have done it alone." Annie offered her friend a tight smile. Her mind was still on the phone call.

Mary Beth leaned toward her friend. "Are you doing OK? You seem preoccupied."

Annie filled her friend in on everything that had happened, knowing full well that the entire Hook and Needle Club would know before the day was over. Some people said Mary Beth was nosy and gossipy, but Annie always thought that Mary Beth passed news around not to gossip, but to share and build support.

Mary Beth helped Annie load the supplies into her

Malibu. Annie drove to the park and sat at a table, eating the tuna sandwich she had prepared. In the distance, waves broke on the rocks. Even with the sun going down, the air had cooled only slightly. Spring weather in Maine was sort of a whiplash experience, cold and rainy one day, and warm with clear skies another. The season when summer fought its way free of winter was called spring.

Annie took a bite of her sandwich and enjoyed the smell of brine in the air. This was going to be a good evening.

Her cell phone rang. "Yes?"

"Hi, Annie, Katrina here. Are we all set?"

"I think so. I'll be up there in just a little bit."

"The ladies are so excited." There was a pause while Katrina murmured something to a person presumably passing by. Annie heard Katrina's soft, easy laugh, and then she came back on the line. "I was going to suggest that since the dining room is at the back of the facility, it might be easier for you to unload if you come into the employee parking lot."

"Thanks, Katrina." Annie hung up.

After running a few more last-minute errands, Annie turned onto Elm Street with a strong sense of excitement building in her. The air had just begun to cool as she drove up to Seaside Hills. The employee parking lot was not as well lit as the main parking lot. At this hour, after dinner, it held only five cars.

After parking, Annie grabbed one of the bigger boxes from the back of the car and shut the door by slamming it with her foot. Through the wide glass doors of the dining room, she could see that Katrina had laid out piles of pattern books and yarns and fabrics that the older women must have had on hand. Katrina had even set up a welcome sign and balloons. A table with refreshments and a punch bowl was also prepared. A sense of lightness and anticipation filled her as she looked at the trouble Katrina had gone to. Through the glass of the door, everything looked ready, but there was no Katrina in sight. When she tried the door, it was locked from the inside.

No problem. Katrina had probably just stepped out for a minute. She set down the box and turned to get another load. Annie stopped abruptly. A shadowy figure stood by her car, peering into her windows.

〜 12 〜

Annie froze in place. Waning light and distance made it hard to discern any features on the man who continued to look into her car. He wore a deep-billed baseball cap. Had this man followed her? She was far enough away and hidden in the shadows of the roof overhang that he might have assumed she had gone inside.

Annie summoned her courage. This was her chance to get to the bottom of this whole thing. A chill came over her even as her hands grew clammy.

Despite the fear, Annie strode across the lot. "Hey, that is my car."

"Is it really?"

She curled her hands into fists. Her heart beat at an intense tempo.

The man strode toward her. He was tall with hunched shoulders. When he came within a few feet and loomed over her, Annie almost turned to run.

The man angled sideways back toward the car. "This is a Chevy Malibu, isn't it?"

Annie nodded, unable to speak.

"Years ago, I had an older model. That baby purred like a kitten. I loved driving that thing out on the coastal roads. Sweet."

Annie relaxed. This could not be the culprit who had

been watching her. This man had a Jimmy Stewart quality to him in both voice and demeanor. "My husband got it for me when we owned a dealership. For sentimental reasons, I just can't bring myself to get rid of it."

"I understand about that. I regret selling my Malibu." He held out a gnarled hand. "I'm Ambrose Stillwater, by the way."

Ambrose offered Annie a strong handshake. "Do you live here?"

"Yup, just out for my evening constitutional." He pointed toward the edge of the parking lot; she inferred there was a walking trail that led into the forest. "So are you here for the big yarn and fabric to-do?"

Yarn and fabric to-do? Only a man would come up with that description. "You've heard about us?"

"My wife Frieda can't stop talking about it."

The door opened and Katrina shouted. "Annie, I'm here. I just had some last-minute details to deal with."

"You are welcome to join us, Mr. Stillwater."

"Delighted to be invited, but this really is a ladies' thing. I appreciate your giving my wife such an opportunity." After tipping his baseball cap to her, Ambrose ambled through the parking lot and around the corner.

Katrina hustled toward Annie's car. "Let me help you with those. Sorry, I wasn't here. The Wii fitness group meets in the rec room tonight. I had to make sure everything was set up for them."

Annie placed a box in Katrina's hands.

Katrina lifted a crochet pattern book off the top of the box. "Looks like we are going to have more than enough sources of inspiration."

"And Mary Beth said she could offer a 20 percent discount for any materials they purchase from A Stitch in Time." Annie grabbed a canvas bag filled with yarn.

They walked across the parking lot. Annie held the door for Katrina. The butterflies fluttered wildly in Annie's stomach as she stepped into the well-lit dining room. Frieda stood close to a table with fabric spread out on it. The older woman had dressed in a stylish denim jacket studded with rhinestones. Her dangling earrings and matching necklace sparkled beneath the lights.

"Are we ready to get started?" Frieda clapped her hands together.

Viola whirled in with a silver tray containing some finger foods.

Frieda put a hand on her hip and scooted her glasses up her nose. "Viola, did you make your famous canapés?"

Viola was dressed in head-to-toe blue plaid with a shining dragonfly barrette in her blond-white hair. "You know I did, sister. And Estelle has made her to-die-for fudge."

A moment later, Joan came in from the main entrance dressed in a yellow frock with matching shoes and earrings. Annie was sure she had seen that outfit in the Dress to Impress window only a few days ago.

Annie's heart swelled to see the trouble the older women had gone to. How special would it make the girls feel to know that such a fuss was being made over them.

Alice and Peggy came into the room. Emily skipped behind her mother. Lily came in a moment later. For a millisecond the teen's eyes grew wide before she put her sourpuss face back on.

Annie helped Katrina spread out the pattern books. She moved to a second table to set up the yarn samples.

Alice sidled up to her friend. "Let me give you a hand with that." She leaned close and whispered, "They really made a big deal out of this."

A girlish giggle escaped Annie's lips. She glanced toward the door just in time to see Mackenzie and Vanessa come in with Kate. The teens had their heads bent toward each other, talking and giggling. Erin trailed behind, shoulders hunched, head lowered. Annie was glad that Vanessa and Mackenzie had become friends, but it sort of left Erin out in the cold.

"I think I'd better go help Erin assimilate," Annie said.

Annie paced across the floor, but before she could get to Erin, Frieda had already bolted across the floor and was complimenting Erin on the sparkling pin she wore on her brown jacket. Annie shook her head. Sometimes all you had to have in common was a little sparkle.

Frieda took Erin's hand and led her toward the treats table, introducing her to Estelle, who had just laid out a tray of fudge.

Alice wrapped her arm through Annie's. "Are you seeing what I am seeing?"

Annie studied the room. Stella had come in. Gwen and Taylor stood at the entrance, the last two to arrive. "What do you mean?"

"Five older women. Five girls," Alice said.

Annie scanned the room. "But there are only four older women."

"Oh please, do you think you are going to be able to

pull Stella and Lily apart?"

"They could pair up, one older with one younger. Each pair could come up with a layette design doing whatever they do best. It would make coordinating things a lot easier."

Alice pointed a finger at her friend. "Exactly."

"I was so worried about everything coming together. God does have a way of working these things out. Gram used to always say that."

Katrina, who had been standing close, draped her hand over the two women's shoulders. "I think that is a great idea. I'll announce it right now." Katrina clapped her hands twice, which caused the murmuring to die down. She welcomed everyone, introduced each older woman by name, and then had Annie introduce each of the teen girls. "So what we want to focus on now is getting to know each other, finding a partner to work with, and coming up with a design plan for the layettes."

The other members of the Hook and Needle Club mingled among the circle of chairs, making suggestions. Erin settled in beside Viola, who had sat down to crochet. Annie took a chair opposite the two where she could look through a pattern book that interested her.

Erin hunched her shoulders and leaned toward the older woman. "What are you working on?"

"Do you crochet, dear?"

"We had a lesson on it, but I am not very good."

"Oh, I bet you do just fine." She patted Erin's leg before focusing on her hook. "I'm just trying to work out some ideas, some stitch combinations." Viola winced.

"Is something wrong?" Sympathy flooded Erin's voice.

Viola let her hook and yarn fall into her lap. "It's this arthritis. I have all these ideas and patterns in my head. I can see how they should come together." Viola held up her hands, frustration rising in her voice. "I just can't get these fingers to do what I want."

Erin took the older woman's hand in her own. "You have beautiful hands."

The older woman's features took on fresh light. "Really?"

"Of course. Your hands know so much." Erin held the small vein-ribbed hand between her palms. "Your hands have done a thousand different things."

Viola held her free hand out at arm's length. "I have wise hands?"

"They know way more than my hands. My hands are flexible, but clumsy."

Viola tapped her forehead with a finger. "The old noggin still works good." She curled her fingers toward her palms and let out a heavy sigh. "But the hands leave a little something to be desired."

Annie looked up from her pattern book. "Erin has a really good artistic sense. And an adventurous streak when it comes to color."

Erin turned to face Viola. "I have an idea. What if I take your hook, and you can talk me through what you want done? We'll use your brain and my hands."

"That just might work." Viola handed Erin the hook and yarn, and talked Erin through a few stitches.

"Look, I'm doing it," Erin said. "This is the best I have ever done."

Frieda sat down on the other side of Erin, holding some yarn and needles.

"Frieda, this young lady will be your hands if you like. She is quite good."

Erin held up the crocheting she'd done, so far obviously pleased with her work. "No really, I am not very good. It's just that it is easier when you talk me through it, and I think of them as your hands."

Frieda waggled the skein of yarn in the air. "I'm going to be adventurous and try my luck with knitting."

"Frieda does beautiful needlepoint," Viola added.

"Oh really? I always wanted to learn needlepoint." Erin chatted animatedly with the two women.

Annie rose to her feet. Mackenzie and Joan were sorting through fabric samples.

Annie held up a dainty blue floral print. "Have you ladies come to some kind of decision?"

"We're going to do a baby quilt and have squares with my cross-stitch on it," said Mackenzie.

The evening lasted for another two hours. Erin conversed with each of the Seaside crafters, moving around the room with ease. She wasn't staring at the floor at all, and she smiled more. She looked more comfortable than any of the other girls.

Annie shook her head. "You just never know."

As the event drew to a close, the Hook and Needle Club group said goodbye and drifted away until only Annie, Alice, and Taylor remained. The Seaside residents cleared away the remainder of the refreshments.

After answering a phone call, Katrina excused herself to

deal with some minor emergency, promising to return.

Alice helped Annie put the supplies back in the boxes.

"Taylor, do you have a ride home?" Alice set her purse on a table.

"I'm supposed to call my mom. We were so busy. Guess I just forgot."

"I can give you a ride." Alice straightened and massaged the small of her back. "If that would be OK."

"I'd like that."

"You seem kind of quiet tonight. Did everything go OK with the project planning?"

"Yes, I am going to work with Estelle." Taylor held up a picture in one of the pattern books. "We're going to crochet a hat, booties, blanket, and jacket."

"I'm glad to hear you connected with someone," Alice said.

"I think all the ladies wanted to work with Erin." Taylor shoved her hands in her pockets and kicked at the floor. "She really hit it off with all of them."

Alice picked up a box and headed toward the open door. "She did seem to be having a good time."

Taylor also grabbed a box and followed Alice through the door.

Annie loaded both boxes in the back of her car. When she stood up, Taylor was staring at the ground. "Is everything all right?"

"You really didn't seem like yourself tonight," Alice added.

Taylor shrugged.

"Is it something that happened here?" Annie cupped a hand on Taylor's shoulder. It was almost as if Erin and

Taylor had traded personalities.

Taylor crossed her arms and stared at the night sky. "No, I had a good time."

Annie studied the teen's face. "We're just used to seeing you be more lively. What happened, Taylor? What is going on?"

Taylor let out a breath. "At school today, I found out that I am eligible to go on this trip to D.C. Because of an essay I wrote, I am a finalist in a contest."

"Taylor, that is wonderful," Alice gushed.

"The trip helps you make connections at a college down there. They pay for your expenses while you are there, but you have to come up with airfare. I don't even want to ask my mom. I know we don't have the money to send me, and there isn't enough time to do fundraising."

"I'm so sorry." Alice's voice broke. "If I had a million dollars, I would give it to you."

Taylor waved her hand in the air. "I'll get over not being able to go. It's just that I get good grades. I want to go to college, but I don't know how I would pay for it. Mom and Dad barely have money for food."

"I am learning that these things have a way of working themselves out, Taylor," Annie said as they walked back toward the dining room.

Alice offered the teen a hug. "Come on, kiddo, I'll take you home. Maybe we can stop for ice cream on the way. I parked out front. See you, Annie."

Annie picked up the final box to take out to the car, listening to the echo of the two women's footsteps on the linoleum floor.

Katrina came back into the dining room. "I can finish up the last little bit of cleanup. You have done enough already."

After giving Katrina a goodbye hug, Annie made her way across the parking lot and set one more box in the back seat. Annie turned, studying the dark, empty lot.

She clicked open her door and sat behind the steering wheel. Tomorrow she would talk to the owner of the Maplehurst Inn. Maybe she would get some answers that would bring this whole thing to a close. She sighed. When she had decided to do the right thing and get the stock back to its owner, she had no idea what she was signing up for.

~ 13 ~

Wally and Douglas showed up the next morning while Annie was getting ready for her brunch at the inn.

The two men stood on her porch, backlit by the early morning sun.

"Sorry to show up unannounced, Annie" Wally ran his hands through his hair. "But we have a couple of hours before we have to be back at that job across town."

"I thought I would test the electrical current in the library before we finish the plastering," Douglas added.

"I can fit some of those shelves," Wally said. "Got the scrollwork all drawn on the oak board. Just have to get it cut out. We'll set up on your patio, if that's all right?"

"Sure, that would work." Annie wrapped her hands around the mug of coffee she'd prepared. "I won't be here for long. I have another commitment."

"That's all right. Like I said, we just have a couple of hours before I need to get across town. We'll lock up when we leave."

As unobtrusive as Wally had been, she was so looking forward to the day this construction job would be done.

After telling the men to help themselves to coffee, she straightened the upstairs and then wiped down the counters in the kitchen. She stared out the window at the flagstone patio. Wally had created a worktable out of sawhorses and plywood so Douglas could use a jigsaw to cut out the scroll work that would be placed on the front of the bookshelves.

The sight of the tulips pushing their way through the earth cheered Annie. The azaleas would be blooming soon too. Gram had planted so many perennials. Yet another legacy Betsy had left behind. Summer would be here soon enough. That made the notion of returning to Texas less appealing. True, she was weary of all that had happened because of the stock certificates, but she couldn't picture herself anywhere but in Stony Point for the summer. She rinsed a dish in the sink, enjoying the feel of the warm water.

When she looked out the window, she saw Douglas pushing buttons and shaking the jigsaw. Then he ran his hands over the wood on the worktable and scratched his head.

Wally poked his head in the kitchen. "Doug says all the electrical is shipshape in the library, and the shelves are a perfect fit."

"That's good to hear." Annie looked back out at Douglas, now struggling to put sandpaper on a sander. "How much carpentry experience does Douglas have? He looks a little lost."

Wally came to the window. "Douglas is a great electrician. He came to me looking for work at just the right time. I kept him on because I think the guy could use the money. He's pretty teachable."

Annie nodded. "As long as you feel he is being a help."

"Oh, he is. The job across town involved a huge amount of rewiring, way more than your library and beyond my expertise. Douglas was a great help."

"I have to get going. Please make sure everything is locked up when you leave."

"You got it, Annie"

Once she was in her car, Annie dug through her purse to find the napkin Ian had written the inn owner's name on. Today she was meeting Linda Hunter. She studied Ian's precise lettering. He'd written the information with such care. Without knowing why, she folded the napkin carefully and placed it in the zippered pocket of her purse for safekeeping.

Annie arrived at Maplehurst Inn with Friday brunch in full swing. The walls of the room had maple wainscoting and framed black-and-white historical photographs of various buildings around Stony Point. Huge west-side windows looked out on a stand of trees with rocks and benches strategically placed. Most of the tables were already occupied. Stella, Gwen, and Alice ushered her over to the table in the center of the room.

"The buffet is to die for," said Alice as she pulled a chair out for Annie.

Annie spotted Ian across the room, though he seemed engrossed in a conversation with two men in suits. She glanced around, trying to guess at who Linda Hunter was.

"Do you guys know what the owner looks like?"

Alice and Gwen shook their heads.

"She has dark hair." Stella craned her neck around. "I don't see her."

Alice said, "Well, let's eat. The crowd should thin out soon enough. We might as well enjoy the good food." Annie chose from a selection of quiches, hash browns, sweet rolls, breakfast meats, and fresh fruit.

The women chatted about Thursday night and the plan to have the older women come to the Wednesday afternoon teen class.

Annie noticed a woman in a black satin jacket approach Ian's table. The woman's dark brown hair was twisted up into a bun secured with chopsticks.

Ian spoke to the woman and then pointed in Annie's direction.

"That must be her," said Annie, tilting her head in the direction of Ian's table.

"Yes, that's Linda." Stella dabbed a napkin on either side of her mouth.

The woman made her way toward them, stopping at several tables to chat.

Annie's heart fluttered a little as she glanced around the room.

The woman arrived at their table. "As if you haven't guessed by now, I'm Linda Hunter."

Annie gestured toward an empty chair beside her. "Do you have time to talk?"

Linda took the seat. "Ian tells me you are trying to track down a woman who stayed here years ago. I've only recently become the owner, but I managed the place for years."

"Yes, what can you tell us about Joan Whitlock?"

Linda glanced at the other women at the table.

"It's OK; these ladies are my friends." Annie introduced them.

Linda picked up a fork and twirled it mindlessly. "Like I said to Ian, I racked my brain trying to remember some details about Joan Whitlock. I've been here for a long time, and the guests start to run together in my head."

"I can understand that." Annie leaned a little closer to Linda, pushing down the fear that she wouldn't garner any meaningful information.

Linda placed the fork on the table and raised her index finger. "However, Joan stayed for such a long time, it's a little easier to remember some things. She was such a nice woman."

"Did she see anyone while she was here?" Alice stabbed a strawberry with a fork.

Linda shook her head. "Her daughter came and stayed with her for part of the time."

"Her daughter?" Annie tried to process what Linda had just told her.

"I'm sorry I don't remember the daughter's name. It was mostly Joan that I visited with. The daughter was very pretty like her mom, and she was pregnant."

Annie's breath caught in her throat. "Pregnant?"

"That is something," said Alice, resting her elbows on the table and leaning forward.

Annie swallowed. This was indeed a surprise. "Her pregnant daughter was with her?" She shook her head.

"Just for part of the time. First Joan came, and then the daughter showed up about a week later."

"How far along was she?" Gwen asked.

"The daughter was a petite little thing. It's hard to tell with women like that. I would guess the third trimester," Linda said.

"Did Joan say why she was in town? Had she come to visit Betsy Holden?"

Linda shook her head. "She mentioned going to visit Betsy, but I never got the impression that was why she was here."

At least that confirmed one of Annie's theories.

"How old was the daughter?" Gwen placed her fork on the table. "Was she a teenager?"

"No, older. I'd say she was at least in her early twenties." Linda patted her hair at the temple. "Why is this so important?"

Annie explained about finding the stock certificates in the attic, her search for the owner, and her belief that Joan Whitlock was the woman she was looking for.

Linda looked up toward the kitchen entrance. "Oops. My chef is signaling me." She rose to her feet. "She never said anything about buying stock certificates. I really didn't talk to her that much, and when we did talk, it was about shopping and needlecraft. I wish I could help you more."

"Actually, you have helped quite a bit already." A pregnant woman traveling that close to the time she was going to give birth seemed odd. Both Joan and her daughter must have had a compelling reason to come to Stony Point.

Linda pushed her chair back under the table. "One more thing I could do is look through some old photographs. It will take a while to dig them out, but I used to take pictures of the dining hall from time to time when it was full. Joan might have been in one of the pictures. I would know her when I saw her."

Alice sat her fork down on the table. "A picture would be really helpful."

Linda made her way across the crowded dining room

toward a panicked-looking man in a white apron standing by a swinging door.

"I would say that was a step in the right direction. We know a little more about Joan than we did before." Gwen adjusted her half-glasses so she could read the check the waitress had just set on the table.

Annie mulled over the new information. "I just wish I could figure out why they were staying in Stony Point. That might be the key to everything."

"Maybe she came here to have her baby," Stella mused. "And maybe she was going to give her baby up—" Stella folded her napkin and laid it precisely on the table.

Gwen shook her head. "People go to Portland to do that sort of thing."

"That's true," said Stella, fingering the brooch on her jacket.

"If it was a problem pregnancy, Stony Point Hospital doesn't have any special facilities," said Alice. "They would have gone to Portland for that too."

Annie nodded. "So the reason they were in town was not connected with the baby the daughter was going to have. It's risky to travel that late in a pregnancy anyway."

"I bet her daughter was the Therese Marie Gilkerson that the stock certificates were intended for." Alice pushed the last bite of a pancake around on her plate to soak it in maple syrup. "Can we safely assume that?"

Annie's thoughts jumbled together. The more she talked, the more uncertain she became. "But she was here with her daughter. Why hide the stock certificates? Why not just give them to her? That editor I talked to in New Hampshire said Joan acted like she was trying to wipe out her identity."

"You mean like she was trying to run away?" Gwen suggested.

"Or trying not to be found, afraid of something or someone." Even as she spoke, Annie could feel her frustration rising.

"Or," Alice raised a finger, "she did something illegal and was trying to hide."

"We have no way of knowing the answers to any of these questions until we find her," Annie said.

Gwen gasped and put her fingers to her mouth. "What if this Joan person lives right here in Stony Point, but she has changed her name and is afraid to come forward?" Her voice took on a conspiratorial tone.

"There might be a Joan among us." Alice slammed her palms on the table, leaned forward and narrowed her eyes at Stella. "Stella, are you or have you ever been a Joan?"

"Oh, stop." Stella fluttered her hand in front of her face and laughed.

Annie appreciated Alice's effort to lighten the mood, but this new information was perplexing. Had she passed Joan in the street and not even known it? If Joan had a reason to disappear, that would explain why she hadn't come back for the certificates.

"Ladies, it is a beautiful day out there," Alice piped up. "I don't want to waste it by staying inside."

Gwen tossed her napkin on the table. "I agree. After all this rain, a day of sunshine should be enjoyed. Let's go for a walk down to the shore."

"That sounds like fun," said Annie.

"I'm afraid I will have to bow out. Jason is picking me

up in a few minutes." Stella pushed her chair back. "I've got some preparations to do for the quartet. Lily is going to be my special guest for the performance."

"You two have really hit it off." Alice dug in her purse and pulled out two dollars, which she set on the table for a tip. The other women did the same.

"She's a sweet girl." Stella nodded as she gathered up her clutch purse and placed her tortoiseshell sunglasses on her face. The older woman walked regally out of the dining hall, head slightly tilted toward the ceiling.

Gwen, Alice, and Annie left the inn and strolled down Maple Street, turning on Grand Avenue. The beach and Butler's Lighthouse came into view. Though it wasn't yet warm enough to put their feet in the water, they took off their shoes so they could feel the sand between their toes. A boy flying a kite shaped like a bird was running along the shore. A man jogging with a dog at his heels passed them by. The women settled down to watch the boats on the water. Several sailboats stayed in the harbor, while the larger fishing boats headed out to sea. The boats moved languidly across the smooth water.

Annie pushed her toes deep into the sand. She enjoyed the feel of the breeze tousling her hair and caressing her face, but any sense of calm was elusive. The more she learned about Joan and the stock certificates, the more anxious she became. When she had found the stocks, she'd pictured a happy ending reuniting the valuable stock with its grateful owner. But now she couldn't help but think that she was about to uncover some long-buried secret that she didn't want to discover.

～14～

By Wednesday morning, Annie felt a renewed sense of anticipation. Today the Seaside women would be coming to the teen meeting. But this time her excitement didn't come with any butterflies. Everything was going smoothly. While the projects were being completed, she could shift her focus to pulling together the presentation ceremony at the Stony Point Hospital. Alice had already started to set things up with her client who worked at the hospital.

She found herself not wanting to think about the stocks and elusive Joan and Therese. All her other plans and good intentions had borne fruit. Positive things were happening because she had trusted her instincts in pulling this intergenerational project together.

Annie had just settled down to work on her own contribution to the hospital project when the phone rang.

"Hello."

"Annie, it's Mary Beth." She sounded out of breath. "We have a problem at the store." Preparing for the worst, Annie slumped down on the couch. Just when she thought things were going so well. "What happened?"

"All this cold weather followed by hot weather caused a pipe to burst in the back room. I've closed the store for the day while the plumber is here. Kate and I are going to move as much as we can out of that back room to prevent mold damage."

Sympathy washed through Annie. Poor Mary Beth. So much to deal with. "I am sorry to hear that. Do you need some help?"

"I think Kate and I have it under control, but we will either have to cancel the Wednesday class or find a different place to meet."

"You let me handle that end of things." Annie paced the floor, her mind already filling with a to-do list. "I don't want to cancel. Maybe we can reroute it to Seaside Hills? Gwen and Alice can probably give me a hand with calling everyone."

"As soon as you know what the plan is, give me a jingle, and I will put a note on the door for anyone who doesn't get the message," Mary Beth said.

Annie hung up the phone and called Katrina at Seaside.

After Annie explained the situation, Katrina responded, "Unfortunately, the dining room is spoken for by the Sons of Scotland Club. I have already made arrangement for transportation for the ladies. If we can come up with an alternative location, I can get the ladies there."

Impulsively, Annie said, "How about my house? Between the living room and the dining room, it's big enough." She'd just have to close the door to the library.

"That sounds like a great idea." Katrina took down the address.

After hanging up, Annie gazed around the living room, hands on her hips. Why did the house always look messier when you thought about having company? Construction in the library had produced extra dust, and the men had tracked in mud from the patio.

After calling Mary Beth and Alice—to get the phone relay started—with the change of location, Annie mopped and dusted, and then grabbed her coat and darted out the door to get some snacks at Magruder's.

Annie pulled into a parking space by the grocery store. Across the street, Mary Beth had already posted a note on the door of A Stitch in Time. Only one light was on and the "Sorry, We're Closed" sign was propped in the window.

"Hey, Annie."

Annie glanced up to see Peggy just as she crossed the street to talk to her. The Cup & Saucer looked dark as well.

"Don't tell me. Water damage."

"Mary Beth's place and The Cup & Saucer share the same plumbing. The damage isn't bad. My boss thinks he can get things cleaned up by dinner. You know what this means." Peggy rocked back and forth on her tennis shoes, excitement gracing her features. "I can come to the class today. I saw the note on Mary Beth's door. Meeting at Grey Gables should be fun."

"I think it will be nice to have a house full of people," Annie said. "I need to start making use of all the square footage I've been blessed with."

Peggy gazed skyward as a few drops of rain fell. "Gotta run home and put Wally's dinner in the cooker and get the neighbor to watch Emily." Peggy raced toward her car, shielding her eyes from the sprinkle of rain.

Annie darted into the grocery store and pushed the cart

through the aisle at a trot. The rain was coming down in buckets by the time she loaded the groceries in her car and raced home.

Annie worked at whirlwind speed to get some snacks together. She had just diluted and mixed the concentrated juice when the doorbell rang, announcing the arrival of the women. Rain slashed against the windows while half the women found a place in the living room and the other half settled around the dining room table.

Annie leaned against the door frame, arms crossed, listening with satisfaction to the chatter and laughter. This is what Grey Gables was for, to be a place of hospitality. Gram had always made sure everyone in town knew they were welcome at her home. She needed to renew that tradition. It didn't make sense for one person to be wandering around this big house alone. Why hadn't she thought of this sooner?

Heading to the kitchen, Peggy passed by Annie. "You'll never believe it, but Estelle used to work as a waitress at The Cup & Saucer. She retired a little before I started working there."

"No kidding? There are so many neat connections between people that we never know about until we start talking."

"So true." Peggy spoke over her shoulder as she headed down the hallway. "This is fun. We should do it more often."

Peggy slipped into the kitchen. Annie relaxed against the doorway. She closed her eyes. The harmony of voices talking and the laughter was like a song to her.

A shriek and the sound of glass shattering came from the kitchen. Annie's eyes shot open. Both rooms fell silent.

Remembering the previous break-in, Annie raced down the hall.

Peggy stood in the middle of the kitchen. All of the color had drained from her face. Pieces of shattered glass scattered across the floor. Annie rushed to her friend, draping her hands on her shoulders and following the line of Peggy's gaze. "Peggy? What happened?"

Peggy cleared her throat and pointed toward an open cupboard door. "A mouse."

Footsteps pounded down the hall. Annie craned her neck in the direction of the doorway where several of the women and teens had gathered. A sinking sensation invaded her limbs as she glanced back at the open cupboard door.

"He stood up on his hind legs and wiggled his nose at me." Peggy's voice wavered.

Heat rose up in Annie's cheeks. "I've been trying to get rid of them."

Behind her, Taylor giggled, but the other women looked even more stricken than Peggy.

"It's just a mouse, guys." Taylor seemed amused by the other women expressing fear over something so small.

Annie grabbed the broom and dustpan. "Why don't you go sit down, Peggy? I'll clean this up."

"I didn't mean to scream so loud. I've just never looked a mouse right in the eyes. They are usually scurrying across the floor." Peggy spoke in a monotone as though she were still trying to recover from the fright. She left the kitchen, still shaking her head.

As Annie cleaned, the chatter in the next room resumed, although not as lively as before. Her ire over the evasive mice grew. This one certainly was being bold.

Annie returned to the dining room. "All taken care of." She noticed that no one had touched the snacks she'd brought out. Leave it to a mouse to put a damper on a party.

Peggy poked her head in from the living room. "Estelle remembers Joan and her daughter when they came into The Cup & Saucer."

Estelle stood behind Peggy, holding her knitting in one hand. "She came in quite often. Real nice lady. Good tipper. Impeccably dressed. She wore such nice suits with a silk scarf around her neck." Estelle addressed her next comment to Peggy. "You always remember the big tippers."

Peggy nodded and then turned back toward Annie. "Estelle is pretty sure her daughter's last name was Gilkerson," Peggy added.

"Real sweet gal, kind of quiet. Something had happened to the baby's father. I don't remember what. The craziest thing was—a couple of years later, the daughter came through town all by herself. She came into The Cup & Saucer for lunch, and I recognized her."

"Why was she back in town?"

"She didn't say. We were busy that afternoon. She acted a little skittish, like she was nervous about something. The reason I remember her at all is because later that afternoon, the poor thing went and got herself killed out on the highway."

Annie suppressed a gasp, feeling a sudden light-headedness. "She died?"

"A one-car rollover. It was a pretty big deal. Don't have accidents like that around here that often."

"Really." Annie could barely form a response.

Estelle and Peggy wandered back to the living room. Annie finished the rest of the afternoon in a daze. As they slipped into their rain gear, several of the Seaside residents thanked Annie for hosting. Annie appreciated their graciousness. The mouse-spotting seemed to have affected the joviality of the party. Alice, Lily, Taylor, and Stella lingered after everyone else had left.

"Look what we have done so far." Lily handed Annie a delicately knitted blue hat with yellow trim.

Annie brushed her hand over the soft yarn. What Stella and Lily had done together was far better than what they could have done separately. "Really beautiful."

"Come along, ladies." Warmth permeated Stella's voice as a glow of affection filled her eyes.

"Stella's dropping us off at my place," Taylor said. "Lily is going to stay the night."

"That sounds like fun," Annie said.

Annie waited until the last three guests exited and the door eased shut before collapsing on the couch beside Alice. "So was that a success or a total disaster?"

"The reviews are mixed." Alice sighed and leaned against her friend's shoulder.

"I am going to take this house apart board by board to find that mouse."

"Don't shoot off your nose to spite your face," Alice said. "I kind of like Grey Gables in one piece."

"What a day." Annie moved her crochet project to the table by the couch. "What do you think about what Estelle said?"

"Memory isn't a perfect thing, but what she said is

probably true. You remember things like a fatal accident. It was probably front-page news in *The Point*." Alice sat up. "We can check Mike Malone's collection of old editions."

"Do you suppose Joan had a reason for staying away, but Therese was able to come back once Joan told her about the stock certificates?" Annie groaned. "I am tired of thinking about all this. All I can do is guess."

"Therese not knowing about the stock certificates would explain why there was a delay in her coming back."

"If she is dead, our only hope is to find Joan." Annie fluffed one of her pillows and looked around the room. "Do you think anyone will ever want to come to my house again?"

"Sure they will. It was just a little mouse." Alice sat up straighter. "I've got to get back to the house. The UPS man brought three boxes of Princessa jewelry today. I have to sort through it all and put it in bags for delivery." Alice rose to her feet. "Try to get a good night's sleep."

Annie stood up as well. "You are a good friend."

After saying goodbye to Alice, Annie made herself a light dinner. Every time she had to open the cupboard where Peggy had seen the mouse, fresh anger surged through her. The pure arrogance of standing on hind legs and wiggling his little pink nose. Did he think he was being charming?

The way things were going, that mouse would run her off before she got rid of him. She knew, too, that it was entirely possible it wasn't just one bold mouse she had to get rid of. A mouse family might have taken up residence. Grey Gables would be reduced to a pile of toothpicks, and she still wouldn't be able to find him, his family, or his nest.

Annie walked through the kitchen, stopping to stare out

the window at the patio. The wind had really picked up. Tree limbs were bent from the force, and her poor flowers were drowning. Either Wally or Douglas had left a piece of the cut wood out on the patio. This much rain would ruin it. The wind caught the piece of oak and lifted it. If she didn't get that wood now, she'd be fishing it out of the ocean.

Annie pushed open the kitchen door and raced across the patio. Raindrops pricked her skin like tiny swords. Wind plastered her hair against her face. She hadn't taken the time to grab a coat. This storm was way worse than she had anticipated.

Annie picked up the cutout piece of wood, which was 12 inches wide and maybe 4 feet long. She pulled matted hair from her face. The wind forced her sideways, and her wet clothes clung to her body.

With her free hand, she reached for the doorknob, which didn't budge. She shook and pushed, but … the lock must have latched behind her. She'd have to go around to the front. Annie was shivering by the time she made it around to the porch. Setting the piece of wood on the decking, she reached for the doorknob. Panic invaded Annie's limbs. She was locked out. What was going on here?

She hadn't locked it after the guests left. She jiggled the handle. Heart racing, Annie dashed off the porch. She must have left a first-floor window open somewhere. She would have to get in that way. A light flashed on the second floor.

Annie blinked and swiped the rain away from her eyes. Someone was in her house. Ignoring how cold she was, she dashed around to the family room window. She'd left it open when the temperature had warmed. With the door into the hallway closed, she had forgotten all about the open window.

Finding a rock from the garden to serve as a step, Annie crawled through the window and landed in a heap on the floor. She lay on her stomach, catching her breath.

Slowly, she rose to her feet. Had she seen someone in the house or not? The light had been real, she knew it. She needed to call the police. Annie glanced around the family room looking for anything that might serve as a defensive weapon. Grabbing a tennis racket from the closet, she edged toward the door; her pulse drummed in her ear as she crept down the hallway toward the kitchen and the phone.

She tilted her head, listening. The light had been on in one of the second-floor bedrooms.

A loud knock on the front door made her jump. Annie patted her chest as fear hit her full force, and her heart pounded intensely.

Who is knocking on the door in this weather?

The knock came again, this time more insistent.

Annie grabbed the phone and edged cautiously toward the door.

She cleared her throat, gripping the tennis racket even tighter. "Who is it?"

"Police, ma'am."

That didn't make any sense. She pulled back the curtain by the door to make sure it was the police and not her intruder. Officer Peters stood on the porch in his rain poncho. Taking in a deep breath, Annie opened the door.

"How did you know to come?"

"We had a call from your neighbor." The officer pointed in the direction of Alice's house. "She saw an intruder crawling in through your window."

"That was me."

Cal Peters' gaze fixed on the tennis racket in her hand. "Ma'am, are you all right?"

Annie set down the phone and the tennis racket. She held her trembling hands in front of her face. "I think someone was ... is in my house." Because she'd been operating on pure adrenaline, she hadn't realized until now how afraid she was. She stepped to one side so Officer Peters could come in.

The young officer squared his shoulders. "I can check it out for you."

She was feeling better already. "I think he was on the second floor."

Soaked to the bone, Annie sat on the couch listening to Peters' footsteps on the stairs and then the creak of the bedroom door and more footsteps and shuffling. A chill that started in the marrow of her bones and worked its way outward made her shiver again. She grabbed the afghan she kept on the arm of the couch and wrapped it around her shoulders.

The officer came back down the stairs. "I searched the rooms. I couldn't find anything."

"OK," her voice sounded squeaky. "He must have left."

"Do you think that's what happened?" The officer narrowed his eyes, implying that he didn't quite believe her about the intruder.

Great, now he thinks I am losing my mind. "I know I saw a light on the second floor. And I am pretty sure I didn't lock that front door." Her voice lacked confidence. Maybe she was losing her mind. Maybe she had just imagined the break-ins. She couldn't offer any evidence of the phone call either. Peters had said that the chief was taking this seriously, but all these false alarms didn't make her look good.

"Ma'am. I'm just not comfortable leaving you here alone. Is there someone you can call?"

"In this weather?" He must have picked up on her anxiety ... or he thought she'd gone completely off her rocker and needed supervision.

The officer raised his eyebrows, indicating that he wasn't leaving until she came up with someone to call. Considering she was old enough to be his mom, the scolding look he gave her was somewhat amusing.

At least she hadn't lost her sense of humor through all this. Annie shivered. She really needed to get out of these wet clothes. "Alice should be available, since she is the one who phoned about an intruder."

Peters put his hands on his hips. "I'll wait while you give her a call."

Annie suppressed a smile at the paternal role the young officer had assumed. Annie obediently picked up the phone.

Even before she could say hello, Alice's panicked voice came across the line. "Oh my goodness, Annie, are you all right? Was there an intruder?"

Annie pressed the phone against her ear. At least her hands weren't shaking anymore. "It's a long story, but I am not feeling very safe right now at Grey Gables. Can I come over to your place?"

"Sure."

"I'll be over in just a minute." The compassion she

heard in her friend's voice bolstered her. After hanging up, she told Officer Peters, "I just need to change into some dry clothes. I think I would like to go over there right away if you could help me make sure everything is locked up tight."

After they checked all of the doors and windows, the officer waited in the driveway until Annie had crossed the short distance to the carriage house and knocked on the door.

She appreciated his vigilance, but it would have been nice if he had believed her.

～15～

Alice opened the door and gathered Annie into a tight embrace. She held her friend for a long moment. "You had quite a scare."

Annie sighed. "On top of everything, I think the police department is starting to think they are dealing with a crazy woman. I *know* I saw a light go on in that window. I *didn't* lock that door. I'm pretty sure someone was in my house."

Alice led Annie into her cozy living room. Bags of various sizes printed with the Princessa or Divine Décor logo were scattered on every flat surface. Alice had a fire burning in her fireplace.

"I tell you what." Annie plopped down in one of Alice's soft chairs. "I cannot get those stock certificates returned fast enough." Her voice broke. "Grey Gables doesn't even feel like the safe, wonderful home Gram intended it to be."

"I don't know about you, but after all this excitement, I'm not tired." Alice poked at the fire. "What do you say I make us some cocoa, and we go over everything you know so far?"

"I suppose that is a good idea." Annie fought off that sinking feeling of despair that threatened to overwhelm her. "I just didn't think returning the stock would be that big a deal. I was trying to do the right thing."

"Talking through everything might get us closer to accomplishing what you set out to do."

Alice was right. Everything was jumbled in her head. "OK."

Alice grabbed a notebook and pen from a desk drawer. "Write down everything you know so far—not speculations and guesses, just what you know for sure. I'll go make the cocoa, and then we can talk this out."

Annie flipped open the notebook. Where to begin? The pen hovered above the piece of paper for a moment. Then she wrote:

The stock is worth a great deal of money.

Joan Whitlock had intended to come back for the stock, but something kept her away.

The stock was issued to Therese Marie Gilkerson.

Because all the records are electronic, having actual physical stock certificates means they were intended to be presented as a gift.

Joan was trying to wipe out any paper trail that would make it possible for someone to find her.

A pregnant daughter stayed with her at the Maplehurst Inn.

The daughter came back into town a few years later, and probably died in a car accident.

Alice placed a steaming cup of cocoa on the coffee table beside Annie. "Have a breakthrough yet?"

"Not really." The aroma of the cocoa made Annie's mouth water. She pushed the list toward Alice. "One thing we need to verify: Was it Therese Marie who died in that accident? Plus, we don't know for sure if Therese Marie is

Joan's daughter. Estelle thought the daughter's last name was Gilkerson. She wasn't sure."

Alice tossed the list on the table. "You are forgetting a couple of things."

"What?"

"Someone broke into your house at least twice, and someone left a threatening phone call." Alice raised a finger as she counted off each item. "And someone looked through your purse when we were at the needlecraft fair."

Annie smiled. At least Alice believed her. "And that someone must be watching me because they knew I had a stock certificate in my purse. But I don't think they know I put the certificates in the bank, because the break-ins have continued." She thought she had been followed that day, but the certificates had been concealed in the envelope. "I showed it to the Hook and Needle Club. I showed it to John at the bank. I may have taken it out at other times, too, all in very public places."

"Once the infamous Stony Point rumor mill got started, it would have been all over town about you finding some stock certificates."

"That first time I thought someone had been in my house was right after it was public knowledge about the certificates." Annie took a sip of her cocoa. "So now we are into speculation. Maybe Joan did wipe out her identity, and she is living right here in Stony Point. She would have heard the rumors about the stock certificates. Something is keeping her from coming forward, but she could be the one breaking in, trying to get the stock."

"The stock was issued to Therese." Alice tucked her

legs underneath her on the couch. "Therese is the one who could cash it in."

"But Joan would be the one listed as the purchaser of the stock, unless she transferred it, in which case only Therese would have a claim on it. If that is the case, Joan's name wouldn't be on anything. It could be that Joan was going to transfer it after she presented it as a gift. The lady at Ocean Side Partners told me that information about who owned the stock was confidential," Annie said.

Alice took another sip of cocoa. "What don't we know?"

"We don't know what happened to the baby that Joan's daughter was about to have." Annie ran her fingers through her wet hair. "We are assuming that the daughter is Therese Marie Gilkerson. She could be someone entirely different."

"Are you saying it is a leap because they have different last names? But Estelle did say the daughter was married and that something happened to the husband. That would explain it."

"I suppose you are right about that," Annie said. "The other thing we don't know is why they were in Stony Point in the first place. I think that is the key." Annie leaned back, melting into the softness of the couch. "So where does that leave us?"

"You got me." Alice shrugged and took a final swig of her cocoa. "Mike Malone has that collection of old *Points*. We can swing by there tomorrow and look through his newspapers to find out if it was Therese Marie Gilkerson who died in that accident. Mike is an encyclopedia about the local news. He might remember something."

Annie rose to her feet and wandered toward a dark

window. She crossed her arms over her body. "I do know one thing. I will welcome the day I can return those stock certificates to Joan or Therese or whoever has a claim on them." In the distance, the huge silhouette of a dark Grey Gables loomed. "And I can have my house back."

Clutching her empty cup, Alice came and stood beside Annie. "It's still a beautiful house. Betsy made it a place of warmth and welcome, and you have done the same thing."

Annie shook her head. "I don't know about that. From little things like that silly mouse to big things like someone breaking in, it just doesn't feel like it."

Alice wrapped an arm around Annie's back and gave her shoulder a squeeze.

Gratitude welled up in Annie. "Thanks for putting me up for the night." She cast her gaze downward. No matter what, she had friends who were true treasures.

Alice gasped. The mug in her hand fell to the floor.

Annie's head jerked up and followed the line of Alice's gaze. "Oh dear." Her hand fluttered to her neck. A single light in a high window of Grey Gables bounced across their field of vision. The intruder must have gone up to the attic to hide when the police officer searched the second floor. "If that is Joan, I've given her free rein to the whole house."

"She won't find any stock certificates there." Alice bolted across the room. "We need to call the police."

Annie grabbed her friend's sleeve. "OK, but we need to get over there. By the time the police get here, the intruder could be gone."

"What are you saying?"

"I want this settled. I'm tired of my house being Grand

Central Station for a thief," Annie insisted.

Alice shook her head.

"All we have to do is corner her. It's two against one."
Annie glanced out the window. The light in the attic winked
out and then appeared again. "We can call the police on the
way over there. I don't want her to get away."

Alice's eyes searched hers. Slowly, she nodded. "OK."
She grabbed her coat and then raced to the kitchen drawer
pulling something out. When she turned to face Annie, she
was holding a hammer. "It's the closest thing I have to a
self-defense weapon."

"Let's go," Annie said.

Alice handed Annie a jacket she had hung up in the
hallway. The rain had abated, but the sun had set more than
an hour ago. In the dark they dashed across the wet grass,
slowing as they drew nearer the house. They stepped up on
the porch, feet padding lightly. Annie pulled her key from
her pocket and slid it into the doorknob "Are you sure you
want to do this?"

Out of breath, Alice nodded and gripped her friend's
forearm. "I still need to call the police."

Annie turned the key and twisted the doorknob.

Alice stepped back away from the door and looked up.
"The light in the attic is gone. I can't see anything."

"Maybe she has moved back down to the second floor,"
Annie whispered. She eased the front door open, wincing
when it creaked.

Inside, they were greeted by near total darkness. She'd
left a single lamp on in the living room, which allowed her
to make out the outlines of furniture.

Alice pressed her hand against Annie's back, her breathing audible in the silence.

Annie tilted her head. No noise came from the second floor. The pounding of her own heartbeat seemed louder than usual. She paced forward. One step. Two steps. Moonlight shone through the dining room window, washing the china cabinet in a warm light.

Alice hung close as they tiptoed toward the stairs.

A faint thud caused them both to stop. They tilted their heads. It had come from the second floor.

"She has to come down these stairs," Annie whispered. Her mouth had gone completely dry. Her pulse drumming in ears clicked up to high volume. "All we have to do is wait here and grab her."

"Hopefully, the police will get here before that." In the darkness, the faint glow of Alice's cell phone became visible.

An icy chill snaked down Annie's back. What if they wouldn't come? Two phone calls in one night claiming she had an intruder would at least make them move slower this time.

As Alice pressed the keypad, each number beeped like a hammer blow. Alice turned away and spoke in a low whisper. "This is Alice MacFarlane. I am at 1 Ocean Drive. And there is an intruder in this house." Alice paused and then said, "No, I don't want to stay on the line." She clicked off her phone. "Now all we have to do is ... wait."

"Yes, wait." Annie swallowed. She wiped her clammy hands on her jeans.

A scraping noise above them set both of them on high alert.

They'd assumed positions on opposite sides of the stairs. Annie probed her memory, trying to think of what was in the living room or dining room that would make it easier to catch and subdue the intruder. Alice still had her hammer. Where had she dropped the tennis racket? She didn't want anyone to get hurt. All they had to do was detain the woman until the police arrived.

Above them, a door creaked open and a soft-soled shoe landed on the wooden stairs.

Annie's breath hitched.

How long would it take the police to get here? If they came at all.

She couldn't see Alice in the darkness. The faintest tap told her the intruder had stepped down another stair. Moving slowly. The intruder must have turned off her flashlight to avoid detection.

Annie held her breath. Every muscle in her body was tense. Each step of the intruder was like the beat in a funeral dirge as they waited at the bottom of the stairs. She gripped the wooden knob on the banister to steady herself.

The footsteps came a little faster.

A sudden flash of light. Annie raised her hands to her eyes.

They'd been spotted.

The intruder pushed past them. In the dark, Annie reached out, grasping fabric, sensing body heat. As quickly as she had located the intruder, she vaporized. Silence pressed on Annie's ears, and then she detected soft footsteps moving quickly. She pivoted in the direction of the noise, crashing against another body.

Alice screamed. Something thudded against the floor. The hammer.

Annie collapsed to the floor. She scrambled across the carpet until she felt the leg of a table she knew had a lamp on it.

She clicked on the light just in time to hear the back door open and the intruder race out into the night.

"Alice." Annie's voice faltered.

"Yes." Alice was out of breath.

Shock had spread through her, making her legs wobbly. "I couldn't see real well, but I'm pretty sure our intruder was a man, not a woman."

The flashing lights of the police siren appeared in the front window.

~ 16 ~

*I*t was midmorning by the time Annie and Alice were finished giving their statements to Chief Edwards at the police station. With Alice to verify that someone had been in her house, the chief and Deputy Peters were taking the investigation very seriously. Cal Peters had stayed at her house to dust for fingerprints. Chief Edwards had assured her that it would take at least a week to process the prints they had found.

Alice and Annie walked out of the police station.

Despite a lack of sleep, Annie's thoughts raced. "The more involved I become with this, the less sense it makes. Who was the man in my place last night?"

"Maybe Joan hired someone to get the stock certificates." Alice pulled a compact out of her purse and reapplied her lipstick. "You did say she was trying to wipe out her identity. Maybe she was afraid of being recognized if she came back to Stony Point."

Annie shook her head. "If the stock is still in Joan's name, she doesn't need the physical stock certificates to cash them in. Ocean Side Partners would have a record of her purchase. So even if she was in hiding, why would she hire someone to get them?"

"Something else is going on. Something we are missing." Alice groaned and shook her head. "I can't think straight on an empty stomach. Let's go get some breakfast."

As if on cue, Annie's stomach growled. "Good idea. Malone's will be open by the time we finish eating. We can see if Mike remembers that fatal car crash Estelle talked about."

The Cup & Saucer was nearly empty when Alice and Annie stepped inside. The breakfast crowd had cleared out and the lunch crowd wouldn't start to trickle in for another hour. The women settled into a booth.

Alice scooted her purse against the wall. "So tomorrow is the big day."

So much had happened that Annie had completely forgotten about the ceremony at the hospital. "Yes, I still have some last-minute things to pull together, but it should be quite nice." Tension knotted through her. If only the cloud of everything connected with those stock certificates weren't hanging over her head.

Lisa set menus in front of them. "The cook is in the process of switching the grill over for lunch. I can do salad, sandwiches, or soup of the day, if you want a lunch item."

Both of them ordered the chicken noodle soup and a ham and Swiss sandwich, which Lisa brought out right away. Over lunch, they divided up the calls that still needed to be made for the ceremony to come together.

Alice took a bite of her sandwich. "I will have a little time to swing by the hospital to see if my friend has any questions or needs anything."

Annie sighed. Idly she picked up one of the saltshakers shaped like a cow and twirled it in her hand. "I was going to spend today finishing my contribution to the project and save the running around for tomorrow. But I can't go home until Cal is done looking for fingerprints."

"You can always go to A Stitch in Time to work." Alice pushed her empty plate to one side.

"All my supplies are still at Grey Gables." A heaviness, partly from fatigue and partly over the break-in, settled into Annie's muscles.

Alice offered her friend a wink and pat on the hand. "Let's go see if Mike has the copy of *The Point* we are looking for."

Annie grabbed her purse. A problem always seemed smaller when she did something about it. "Let's go."

They crossed Main Street and entered the hardware store. Mike Malone, perched halfway up a ladder, placed lightbulbs on a high shelf.

Annie approached him. "We need to look something up in your old editions of *The Point*, if that's all right? Do you remember a fatal car crash that took place in the late 1990s?"

Mike stepped off the ladder and rubbed his forehead. "Sure, I think I do." He crossed his arms and stared at the ceiling as though trying to pull the memory up. "That would have been 1998 or 1999 in the spring."

The library had some copies of *The Point*, but they weren't indexed, and they didn't come with Mike's wonderful memory.

Annie smiled. "Thanks, Mike. Let us know if you remember anything else."

"Enjoy your search. Fiona's been in there organizing." He shook his head. "And now she's talking about painting in there."

Annie was heartened to hear that Mike's wife had decided to organize his collection of old *Points*. While she was glad that Mike had taken it upon himself to archive a part of Stony Point history, his "system" wasn't exactly something to write home about. "Follow me," she said to Alice.

They stepped through a pine-paneled door. Though the room was still cluttered with boxes and equipment, it looked as though it had been dusted, and there were labels on the file cabinets.

Annie scanned the file cabinets until she found one that said 1995–1999. *The Point* was not a big paper, usually just one or two folded sheets or a little more if one of the stores was having a big sale or there was some special event in Stony Point. She opened the drawer, pulled out a stack, and handed half to Alice.

Annie found a wooden box to sit on.

Alice cautiously lowered herself into a lawn chair. "I hope this isn't in here because it is broken." She bounced slightly on it to check its stability.

"The accident would probably be front-page news, don't you think?" Annie set the top newspaper, with a lead story about library renovations, to one side.

Alice nodded. "That would be the fastest way to get through this stack."

They both filed through, checking the top page of each edition.

Annie stopped and stared down at the May 15, 1999, edition which featured a photograph of a mangled car. The headline read "Woman Dies in Car Crash."

Annie put her finger on the paper. "Here." She read

out loud. "'A woman identified as Marie Gilkerson died in a one-car rollover.'"

Alice scooted toward her and looked over her shoulder. "It doesn't say anything about relatives or a funeral service."

"She was from out of town. Look, it says here she was from Michigan. Her name and where she was from is information they probably got off her license." Annie stared at the picture of the twisted car.

"That's a long way to come. She left without getting the stock certificates. She must have left in a hurry."

Annie sat back on her box. "The name in the article isn't Therese Marie; it's just Marie."

"Maybe the reporter shortened it or just got it wrong. Plus you know how some people drop their first names and go by their middle names. The important thing is that her last name was Gilkerson."

"I suppose you are right." Annie mulled the information over in her mind. Someone had to have come to claim the body.

"I don't recognize that reporter's name. Mike mostly gets high school students to help him. I doubt he is around anymore."

"He probably wouldn't be able to tell us anything more. Really, it looks like he just worked off the police report." Annie filed through several more issues, hoping to find a follow-up story. "She comes into town. Probably to get the stocks ..."

"She must have found out about the stock two years after Joan left it there," Alice said. "Otherwise, she would have come back sooner."

"That has to be it. Joan must have told her." Annie closed the newspaper and put it on her stack.

Mike stuck his head in the door. "Finding what you need?"

Annie held up the article. "Do you know anything else besides what is in this article?"

Mike tugged on his mustache. "I do remember the state police came down to do an investigation into the cause of the accident."

Alice craned her neck and turned sideways in the lawn chair. "What did they find out?"

"No drugs or alcohol, didn't hit another car or a deer. She was just going way too fast."

"Estelle did say she seemed nervous at the restaurant," Annie said. "Something must have scared her, and made her want to leave town fast." She set the old issue back in the stack. "Do you know who came for the body?"

"That was the saddest part." Mike shook his head. "It's not something you put in an article."

A lump formed in Annie's throat. "You mean no one came."

Mike nodded. The front door buzzed, indicating that Mike had a customer. "Excuse me, ladies."

They both stayed for a moment in the quiet room.

Alice spoke up. "Maybe you were right all along. Joan didn't come back for the body or the certificates because she couldn't come back. Joan is dead too."

Annie tried to ignore the sorrow that welled up inside her over this last bit of news. "I really need to get home and get a nap so I can finish that project. Last night was a long night."

"Let's go then. You can crash at my place if the police aren't gone."

Annie rose to her feet and picked up her purse. "Thanks."

After saying goodbye to Alice, Annie drove to Grey Gables. She was relieved to see that the police car was no longer parked outside. She dragged herself up the stairs and trudged across the porch. She wandered into the living room and collapsed on the couch.

Just a short nap. That was all she needed. Her limbs felt like they were made of lead, and her eyelids were heavy. She had a dozen things she needed to do today, and half the day was already gone. She folded her legs underneath her and rested her head against a pillow.

Yes, she did have a ton to do for the presentation ceremony, but she couldn't do anything if she was exhausted. The fog of sleep filled her brain. She tried to make a mental list of what she needed to get done. Finish the project and call Katrina …

She snuggled her head against the couch pillow and drifted off to sleep. Boots curled up against her stomach.

She awoke to a buzzing sound. Where was that noise coming from? Her thoughts were still trapped in whatever dream she had been having.

Annie sat up, trying to clear her head. It took her a second to realize the noise was the doorbell. Annie stood up, a bit unsteady on her feet.

"I'm coming." How long had she been asleep? She stumbled toward the door. A glance out the window at the graying sky told her that it was early evening. She'd slept for at least six hours. When she opened the door, an older woman dressed in a tailored navy suit stood on her porch.

"Hello, I'm Joan Whitlock. I understand that you have been looking for me." The woman tugged on the sleeve of her suit.

A gentle breeze could have knocked Annie over. "Yes, I—" Annie shook her head. In the light that spilled out from the living room, Annie studied the woman in front of her. Softly etched crow's-feet surrounded her eyes, which were dull with fatigue. She was shorter than Annie. Her shoulders curved slightly forward. Somehow she had pictured Joan Whitlock as being a more sophisticated and intimidating figure. "So you are Joan Whitlock?"

"Yes," The woman wetted her lips. "I know this is kind of a surprise. I have I.D."

Annie pressed her fingers into the door, debating what to do. The person in the house last night had been a man. Was Joan working with him? She hesitated to invite this woman into her home. "So what prompted you to come back now?"

The woman's gaze darted from one side of the porch to the other as though she thought someone might be watching her. "Actually, I am kind of in a hurry. I'm just passing through town."

"Oh really, where from?" She tried to keep her tone friendly. Maybe she wasn't completely processing what had just happened because her head hadn't cleared from deep sleep. Though she had longed for Joan to make an appearance, having her show up now just seemed ... off.

"I drove up from New Hampshire. If you don't mind ..." The woman stepped inside the house and looked around.

"I do really need those certificates."

Annie took a step back. She didn't want to come off as inhospitable, but it had just been last night that she thought Joan was in hiding and breaking into Grey Gables on a regular basis. And just this morning, Alice had speculated that Joan was dead. "How did you hear that I had found the stock certificates?" She struggled to keep the interrogating tone out of her voice.

"I've kept in touch with some people from Stony Point." Joan walked around the living room and picked up the ceramic bird Annie had on the windowsill.

Joan's sudden boldness was off-putting. Annie hesitated at asking her why she hadn't come forward sooner. Questions played at the corner of her mind. She just hadn't been prepared for Joan to suddenly show up on her doorstep.

Joan set the bird back on the windowsill. "So you have the certificates, right?"

"I do have them, but they are in a safe-deposit box at the bank." Turning the certificates over was the answer to all her problems. Why was she dragging her feet?

"Oh, they're in the bank." The woman seemed genuinely surprised. She smoothed the front of her suit and tugged on the hem of her blazer. "Like I said, I am only in town for the day. I suppose the bank is closed by now. I'll have to spend the night. I'd be happy to go with you first thing tomorrow."

Annie glanced up at the clock. Six o'clock. She hadn't realized how long she had slept. "I have a really busy day tomorrow. I am helping with a ceremony at the hospital. It would be something you would be interested in. Some local women and teens have made layettes, using their skills as needlecraft artists." The statement was intended as bait. Annie waited for Joan's reaction.

Joan lifted her chin slightly. "Being an editor of that craft magazine was a lifetime ago."

She certainly knew the right answers. Maybe this was the real Joan. Annie needed to buy some time, consult the Hook and Needle Club, maybe even tell the police. "I have a really busy day tomorrow. I'll get the certificates before the bank closes, but I won't be able to get together with you until after the ceremony."

Joan's cheek twitched slightly. "I suppose if that is the way it has to be."

"I know this is an inconvenience." Annie rested her hands on the back of the couch. "You'll have to stay overnight."

"If that is what we have to do." Again, the woman bristled and then tugged on the sleeves of her suit.

"We could meet at The Cup & Saucer. I can call you when the ceremony is over."

"Why don't we just set a time?" The woman's words were clipped, her tone impatient.

"All right; for sure I will be done by eight o'clock." Annie grabbed a piece of paper and a pen. "I'll be running around quite a bit. I'll give you my cell number in case the plan changes." She handed Joan the piece of paper.

"All right, then." She folded the piece of paper and put it in her purse. "We'll be in touch." She locked gazes with Annie. A moment later, she turned her back toward Annie and headed toward the door.

"Wait," said Annie. "I guess I would like to see that I.D."

The woman pivoted, eyebrows raised, but her voice remained calm. "Certainly." She pulled out a leather pocket-book and flipped it open.

Annie stared at the driver's license for Joan Whitlock. She didn't know that much about I.D., but it looked real. "Sorry, I just felt like I should ask."

Joan flipped the pocketbook shut. "I understand."

Still in a daze, Annie listened to the woman's footsteps echoing on the wooden floor. The door swung open and closed. Annie ran to the window and watched as the woman got into an older model Buick.

She touched her hand to her chest. All she had to do tomorrow was go to the bank and give Joan the stock certificates. This is what she had wanted, to have this whole thing over and done with. But the pieces just didn't fit. Who was the man in her house last night? And why all of a sudden did Joan come forward? Word about the stock certificates had been swirling around Stony Point hours after she had found them. Why would Joan's "friends" wait so long to tell her? It could be that the break-ins had nothing to do with the stock certificates. She shook her head. Somehow, she just knew that all this was connected. She really needed to talk to someone about this.

She phoned Alice, but got no answer. She'd just have to try to find time to call her tomorrow.

Annie picked up her crochet project. She could finish this tonight. As her hook formed the yarn into concise stitches, she worked through what the arrival of Joan meant. She felt unsettled rather than relieved. Joan had the right answers, yet something didn't feel right. It was a small thing, but both Linda Hunter at the Maplehurst and

Estelle had described Joan as being elegant and sophisticated. Maybe the years had chipped away at Joan's sense of style and her personality, but the woman who had come to the door seemed uncomfortable in her suit. When people talked about Joan, she sounded like a woman with a degree of finesse. This woman had come across as direct, almost bossy.

Annie heard a loud crash upstairs. Old fears returned until she realized Boots wasn't in the living room. She ran up the stairs to the attic. The would-be thief had left the door at the bottom of the stairs to the attic open. Annie hadn't even had time to go through the house since the police had been here.

As if the attic couldn't be cluttered enough, it looked as though the culprit had simply become frantic and started emptying boxes and flipping open trunks, even pulling cushions off of couches. Boots came out from behind a stack of old books.

Annie slumped down on the floor. "Find that mouse for me yet?"

Boots sauntered over to her and rubbed against her leg. Annie spent some time straightening the attic and then worked up the courage to check on the second floor, which only had a few opened drawers, though things had been pulled out of her closet. The thief must have done all of this after Officer Peters had checked the upstairs.

She worked until her stomach started to growl. She headed downstairs. The clock in the kitchen read ten o'clock. She had lost even more time, but at least Grey Gables was back to normal—or as normal as it could be, considering.

She fixed herself a cup of tea and a sandwich.

She'd just have to get up early to finish the project. Then she could run to Magruder's and get the food together that she had promised to bring. So much to do.

She had gone up only two steps to the second floor when she realized she didn't feel safe sleeping in her bedroom. Being up there was too much of a reminder of the home invasion that had taken place. Annie grabbed the afghan off the back of a chair and settled back down on the couch, pushing the pillow under her cheek and pulling the afghan up to her chin. The afghan was one that she had made and had always given her comfort when she was sick or feeling blue.

Just as she was drifting off, headlights flashed across the window. Annie sprang up and raced to the window just in time to see a police car going by on Ocean Drive. He'd slowed when he went by Grey Gables. She stood at the window until the taillights faded into the distance.

She lay back down on the couch and squeezed her eyes shut. The last thing she needed was a sleepless night.

～ 17 ～

Annie woke with a start when the sun shone through the living room window, warming her face. She took a quick shower and worked at a breakneck pace to finish the blanket for the layette. It was noon by the time she was ready to go into town to get the baking supplies for her share of the refreshments. She grabbed a large handbag that would hold all of the stock certificates. Annie stared into the empty bag. Maybe by the end of the day, the certificates would no longer be her problem.

After getting the groceries, she ran to the hardware store to pick up the banner Mike had made for her that said "Bringing Generations Together." She swung into Finer Things to see if they had any ideas for last-minute decorating. Annie wandered around the store. Gram had a linen tablecloth, and Alice had promised to bring balloons and a table that she used for her demonstrations. As she wandered the aisles, Annie realized she was procrastinating about getting the stock certificates. She clenched her teeth. She really didn't have time to waste. Steeling her resolve, Annie left Finer Things, crossed Main Street at Oak, and headed into the bank.

The redheaded teller behind the high counter offered Annie a smile. "Good afternoon, Mrs. Dawson. How may I help you?"

"I need to get into my safe-deposit box."

The teller came out from behind the counter. She glanced down at Annie's large bag but said nothing; then she led Annie into the secure room where the boxes were kept. After the teller put her key in the box and then Annie put hers in, she said, "I'll leave you alone."

Annie pulled the box out of its slot and set it on the counter. She stared down at the stack of certificates. She unzipped the bag and set it on the counter. Her hands trembled as she pulled the certificates out.

She zipped the bag shut and headed out the door. She hadn't told Joan she would meet her alone at The Cup & Saucer. The Hook and Needle Club had been with her on this from the beginning. Certainly one of them would be able to come with her to return the certificates. Maybe her perception of Joan was inaccurate, but she needed a second opinion before she gave them up.

Annie swung into A Stitch in Time to make sure everything was all set with Mary Beth. Mary Beth assured her that everything was falling into place. "I'm going to try to get up there early to help you with the decorations." Her glance fell to the large bag in Annie's hand. "Did you decide you needed an even bigger purse?"

Annie bit her lip. Mary Beth was a dear, but she had a tendency to talk. If she told Mary Beth what was going on, the word would be out to the whole town within the hour. Given that having the stock was like a target painted on her back, Annie opted not to tell her the whole story. Alice was the one she felt comfortable talking to. "I just had some extra stuff I needed to carry around today."

Mary Beth eyed her for a moment before turning her attention back to the catalog she was flipping through. "We'll see you later today."

Annie got home and mixed up a batch of Mexican tea cakes. The phone rang just as she put the first cookie sheet in the oven.

Annie closed the oven door and grabbed the phone. "Hello."

Alice's voice came across the line. "I saw on my caller I.D. that you called last night."

"You will never believe who came to my door last night. Joan Whitlock."

A heavy silence filled the line. A moment later, Alice said, "Really? So I guess this means the ordeal is over."

"I'm hoping. It's just that … I don't know … the whole thing seems weird."

"Weird? Do you think this woman is *really* Joan Whitlock?"

"She answered all my questions, and she had a driver's license. She knew all about the certificates and asked for them. I reluctantly agreed to meet her later—to give her the goods. I was so taken off guard by her showing up, and there were a ton more questions I could have asked her. About her daughter, for one." A blast of heat hit Annie when she checked the cookies in the oven.

"Maybe you can ask her more questions tonight before you hand them over to her."

Annie picked up a spatula. "That's what I was think-ing. Then if something seems fishy, I'll call the police. I don't want to use up manpower on another false alarm.

You're a good judge of character. Can you come with me?"

"Sure, I can do that. I've got to get back to my baking," Alice said.

"Thanks, Alice." Annie hung up. The rest of the afternoon went by in a whir. She finished baking. While the cookies were cooling, she placed the layette into a box she had gotten at Finer Things. She secured the treats in containers. After taking Gram's tablecloth out of an upstairs closet where it hung, she loaded everything into the car.

She'd brought the bag with the stock certificates so she could keep an eye on it. She wouldn't have time to come back to the house to get it; the certificates had to come with her. Feeling uneasy, Annie loaded the bag into the trunk of the Malibu and locked it.

When Annie arrived at the hospital, Alice had already set up the table and balloons in the reception area outside the hospital nursery. She greeted Annie with a hug and then pointed to an older woman behind the counter. "Annie, this is my friend Sarah Mortenson."

Sarah, whose most distinct feature was a modified beehive hairdo, waved. "I'm her best Princessa customer."

Alice pulled a roll of streamers out of a bag. "You want to help me hang this? Sarah says we can use the whole reception area."

Sarah came out from behind the counter, joining the two women. "I can lend you a hand. We have two newborns in the nursery. Both moms would love to be a part of the ceremony. This is the neatest thing that has happened in all my years of working here."

Annie stepped up on a chair as Alice handed her a streamer. "Have you worked here long?"

"Twenty years." Sarah patted her big hair. "I've been on this floor for just a couple of years. I do love the babies."

Erin and Viola walked in together. "I know we are early, but I just couldn't wait. Come see what Viola and I made together." Erin lifted a blue-and-yellow crocheted blanket out of the gift bag she was holding.

Annie admired the blanket. The stitching was close to perfect. "Oh, Erin, it's beautiful."

Erin gave Viola a sideways hug. "We did it together." Her face beamed.

"This little lady has so many wonderful ideas," the older woman said.

"Can we help with anything?" Erin put the blanket back in the gift bag.

Annie unrolled a section of streamer. "Alice will put you to work."

While Alice delegated jobs, Annie spread out Gram's tablecloth. Gram had done a delicate cross-stitch floral design in one corner of the linen fabric. She brushed her fingers over the purple pansies.

Peggy and Gwen arrived, each holding a tray of refreshments.

"We are going to need another table," Sarah said. "I think we have one in the basement if you want to give me a hand."

Annie followed Sarah down a concrete stairwell. At the base of the stairs, Sarah flipped on a light and opened a metal door with a small window.

Annie stared around at file cabinets, what looked like a piece of broken medical equipment, and shelves piled with stacks of paper and several coffee machines. "What is this place?"

Sarah walked to a corner and grabbed a card table. "The land that time forgot. We've got some old medical records in the file cabinets and just things people thought they were going to fix and then forgot about." She ran her hand over the table. "This is a little dusty. I'm going to have to wipe it down." She turned back toward the corner. "There is another one over there if you want to grab it."

Annie retrieved the second table. An idea budded inside her head. "How far back do those files go?"

"I'm not sure." Sarah shrugged. "Records less than ten years old are upstairs." She turned her attention to the tables. "I think we have something in the break room that we can cover these with." She hefted the table up the first couple of stairs. "Why did you want to know about the files?"

"I am trying to find out about some women who stayed in this town years ago. One of them was pregnant. If the woman came in for an exam or needed medical attention, there would have been a record of it, right?"

"Sure, do you have a name for the mom?"

"Therese Marie Gilkerson."

"That's not ringing any bells." Sarah went up a few more stairs. "We could probably do a search."

Several bars of classical music spilled down the hallway, punctuated by the sound of women chattering.

"Sounds   like   we   have   quite   a   crowd   already."

Annie's heart fluttered with excitement. When she arrived at the top of the stairs, Stella was arranging a quartet in a corner of the reception area.

The older woman waved. "Hello, dear. I thought a little live music would be nice. I hope you don't mind."

"No, not at all." Annie smiled. Everyone's contribution had added so much to the celebration. "I think that was a great idea."

By the time Annie had set up the tables and arranged refreshments, the place was teeming with people. Alice arranged the layette sets on the second table, placing a flower arrangement in the center of the display.

Ian entered the corridor. His eyes went wide when he saw the crowd. A younger man followed Ian. Her guess— that the young man was the reporter from *The Point*—was confirmed when he took out a camera.

Sarah hooked her arm through Annie's. "My goodness, that young woman over there is very good with the babies."

Annie followed the direction that Sarah was pointing. Erin sat holding a baby surrounded by older women. "Yes, Erin seems to connect with the old and the brand new."

"She has a way of bringing them together."

God has a way of working these things out. As Annie watched Erin, Gram's wisdom floated back into Annie's head.

"You know," said Sarah, "we need volunteers from time to time when we get lots of babies at once." She squeezed Annie's elbow. "I'm going to go talk to her."

Holding a cup of punch, Taylor sidled over to Annie. "This is fabulous." She wore a lacy teal dress that offset her black hair and creamy skin.

A sense of satisfaction and joy filled Annie. "Yes, it's all very lovely."

Ian pulled himself away from the conversation he had been drawn into. He grabbed the young man with the camera and walked over to Annie.

"You have done something wonderful here," Ian said.

"I didn't do it alone," Annie basked in the warmth of his smile.

"It's something that we could make an annual event."

"I hadn't thought about that, but I am sure all the women would love to create more layettes." The idea appealed to her.

"If it's a yearly thing, you'll have to stick around and make sure everything comes together. You'll never be able to go back to Texas." Ian's eyes lit up as he gazed at her.

Annie blushed. "I suppose that's true."

"You've gone and made yourself a permanent part of Stony Point." Ian winked.

"Is that what I've done?"

Ian pointed to the young man with the camera. "That man is Greg Smith. He's busy with photos right now, but he knows who you are. I'm sure he will want to talk to you after things die down."

Ian leaned toward Annie and whispered in her ear. "Since you are responsible for all this organized mayhem, I'm sure you will want to say a few words." He signaled Stella to quiet the quartet as he moved toward a microphone that had been set up in the corner.

Annie froze. She hadn't realized she'd be asked to speak.

Ian grabbed the microphone as the crowd quieted down and looked toward him. "I would like to thank everyone who came today. Bringing generations together is one of the things in which Stony Point prides itself. In creating this project, Annie Dawson has built bridges between senior citizens, teens, and those in between, and created a way for the newest of our citizens to feel welcomed to Stony Point. Annie, would you like to say a few words?" He handed her the microphone.

Annie's heart pounded in her chest. Public speaking had never been her favorite thing, but as she stared out at the crowd, she saw a sea of friendly faces. "I just want to say what an honor it is to be here and to be part of this community. The idea for the intergenerational project may have been mine, but I certainly didn't do it alone. Over and over, people stepped up to the plate and offered their gifts and talent and time. This truly has been a community project, and I'm so grateful for the women from Seaside, the teens, and my friends from Hook and Needle Club, not to mention Katrina, activities director at Seaside Hills Assisted Living." She turned slightly to face Ian. "And our own wonderful mayor."

One of the newborns let out a sweet cry. Everyone laughed.

"And of course, the reason we are here: the babies. So enjoy the food and music, and take a moment to look at the beautiful layettes these women have created and to say 'thank you.' I'm so glad all of you came here today."

After applauding, people gradually returned to visiting and eating.

Greg Smith moved toward Annie. "I'm sure Ian told you I'd like to ask you a few questions."

After snapping a photo of Annie standing beside the display, Greg took out a small notebook. His questions were easy to answer. Then Annie visited some more with the guests and enjoyed the music.

Alice came up behind her and whispered in her ear. "Maybe we should get going. It's quarter to eight."

She'd pushed the meeting with Joan out of her mind, but it had to happen.

Annie stopped to talk to Ian. "Thank you for making this such a success."

Ian's eyes sparkled. "Like you said, it really was a group project."

Annie said goodbye to a few more people. She and Alice made their way out to the dark parking lot.

Before Alice got into her Mustang, she said, "I'll meet you down there."

Annie got into her car and drove down Main Street. She found a parking space a couple of blocks from The Cup & Saucer. She unlocked her trunk and pulled out the bag. Main Street was almost empty at this hour. Her feet tapped on the sidewalk. Across the street, the display lights had been left on in Dress to Impress, but the store was closed.

She didn't see Alice's Mustang. Annie entered The Cup & Saucer. Two older gentlemen sat at the counter and a family occupied a corner table. She could see into the kitchen, where Lisa was joking with the cook.

Annie selected a table that provided a view of the door.

Lisa walked over to her and handed her a menu. "How are you doing tonight?"

"OK, but I'm not really hungry. I'll just have a cup of

hot tea." She hadn't realized her hands were sweating until she handed the menu back to Lisa.

"Mrs. Dawson, are you OK? You look kind of ... anxious."

Was she that easy to read? Annie forced a smile. "I'm all right. I'm just meeting someone, and I don't know how it will go."

Lisa nodded. "I'll bring you that tea."

Annie checked her watch. Exactly eight o'clock. Alice walked in and snapped her cell phone shut. She took a chair kitty-corner from Annie. "Sorry, I had a call from my sister in Florida that I had to take." Alice patted her friend's hand. "It's all going to be over in just a little bit."

"I need some straight answers from Joan before I give her these things." Annie touched the handbag. "For one, I have to make sure she isn't in any way connected to these break-ins."

"Being in sales has helped me read body language pretty accurately. I'd be able to tell you if she's lying."

"That's why I brought you along." Annie took a sip of her tea. "We can get Lisa to get you a cup if you like."

"That sounds delightful."

The two women worked their way through two cups of tea each while they watched the door.

Lisa came out from behind the counter. "Ladies, we close down in fifteen minutes."

Annie's shoulders slumped. "I guess she is not going to show." She folded and unfolded the napkin.

"What are you thinking?"

"It just seems odd. She was so adamant about getting the stock certificates."

Alice scooted her chair back and rose to her feet. "Maybe she *is* involved in something illegal, and she chickened out because she thought you would bring the cops."

The two women made their way across the empty restaurant. "What a day, huh?" Annie sighed. "Filled with ups and downs."

Outside on the sidewalk, the women hugged as they said goodbye. Annie walked down the empty street, suddenly aware of the headlights of a van that peeled away from the curb.

Locking herself in her car, Annie drove through the dark streets of Stony Point, onto Ocean Drive. The light she had left on in the living room of Grey Gables was a welcome sight.

Lugging the big bag with the stocks, she went inside and bolted the door behind her. After slipping into her pajamas, she fell into her bed. Sleep came quickly. She dreamed of Joan standing at her door, reaching out her hand and demanding, "Give them to me."

She was awakened the next morning by her cell phone playing *Amazing Grace*. She stumbled out of bed and rummaged through her coat pockets to find the phone.

"Have you read the paper yet?" Alice sounded out of breath.

"No, is there an article about the ceremony?"

"Not on the first page." Something in Alice's tone sounded foreboding.

"What is it?" Tension knotted Annie's stomach.

"Maybe you'd better just get the paper. I'll be over in a minute."

— 18 —

Feeling uneasy about Alice's phone call, Annie went downstairs and made a pot of coffee before retrieving the paper from her porch. Her steps stalled as she read the headline: "Woman Found Dead on Beach." A photograph of an older-model Buick in an empty parking lot within sight of the ocean dominated the front page. The caption beneath the picture read, "The car believed to belong to the victim."

Annie clutched the paper tighter and kept reading. "A woman identified as Joan Whitlock was found dead in a rocky part of the beach."

Annie fell into a wicker rocker, doubled over with nausea.

"They think she drowned." Alice's voice floated up to her from the walk.

Annie straightened and shook her head. When she tried to finish reading the article, she couldn't focus her vision. "Drowned?"

"The paper doesn't say if it was an accident, or if she jumped in or … something else."

"It just happened last night. The chief probably doesn't know the cause of death yet." Annie struggled to get a deep breath.

"Or they are withholding the information so they can investigate." Alice stepped up the stairs of the porch.

"This doesn't make any sense." Annie shook her head in disbelief. "No one knew she was in town. I didn't tell anyone but you."

Alice collapsed in a wicker chair. "I didn't say a word to anyone."

Through the open door, Annie could hear the phone ringing and the message machine kick on. No doubt the members of the Hook and Needle Club were calling her for an explanation, something she didn't have. Guilt washed through her. Should she have told the police about Joan right away? "Sometimes I think it would have been better if I had just thrown those certificates away when I found them."

Alice draped a supportive hand on Annie's arm. "You can't blame yourself."

"That poor woman." Annie touched her fingers to her chest. "I have to do something."

"Ian might know what is going on. I'm sure he is in touch with Chief Edwards, and they are dealing with things."

"If Ian volunteers information, that's fine, but I'm not going to put him on the spot. I don't want to abuse our friendship in that way."

"I understand."

Annie sat up straight. "There is one thing." The landline rang again. "We've been saying all along if we knew why Joan and her daughter came to Stony Point in the first place, we might have the missing piece of the puzzle."

"Yes?"

"Yesterday at the ceremony, I started talking to your friend Sarah. What if Therese Marie had to see a doctor while she was here? Somebody at the hospital might remember something."

Alice pulled out her cell phone. "I'll give Sarah a call right now."

Annie rose to her feet. "Give me just a few minutes to get ready." She went into the house, glancing one more time at the newspaper article before placing it on a table by the door. Within twenty minutes, Annie was dressed and ready to go.

Alice waited for her at the bottom of the stairs, offering a coffee refill. "It's Sarah's day off. When I told her this was connected to the woman who died, she said she would be glad to meet us at the hospital. Should we take my car?"

"Sounds good." The phone rang a third time. "I sure don't want to stay home listening to that phone ring all day," Annie said.

Within minutes the Mustang pulled up outside the hospital. Annie's sense of urgency increased with every step as she and Alice hurried to the nursery. The reception area that had been so festive yesterday was back to its standard institutional decor. No bright colors, just beige chairs and beige walls.

Sarah, dressed in slacks and a floral-print shirt, stood by the counter. A woman about Sarah's age stood beside her, looking as if she had just been tending her garden. Her jeans had dirt on the knees, and the denim shirt showed signs of wear.

"Annie and Alice, this is Doris."

Doris held out a hand. "I retired from nursing several years ago."

Sarah held up a file folder. "When I pulled the file on

Marie Gilkerson, it didn't ring any bells for me. I was still doing shift in other parts of the hospital, but Doris was pretty much full-time here."

"I remember Marie Gilkerson, and her mother, Joan Whitlock." A note of sadness punctuated Doris's voice.

"So they were mother and daughter," Alice whispered.

"I never quite got the whole story from either one of them, but it was a very tense time for them. Joan's ex-husband lived around Stony Point. When Marie's husband died suddenly, and Marie was about to give birth, they had hoped to convince him to step up to the plate as Marie's father and the baby's grandfather. I don't think the meeting went too well. Then Joan just disappeared one day. Marie was waiting for her mother's return when she went into labor."

A sense of hope returned to Annie. "So she did have the baby here?"

Doris nodded. "After the baby was born, and it seemed that Joan wasn't going to come back, poor Marie was beside herself. I went into her room one night before I got off shift. Marie was crying. She said she couldn't see herself raising the baby alone."

"So she gave the baby up for adoption?" said Annie.

Doris nodded again.

"Were Joan and Marie fighting? Is that why Joan went away and didn't come back?" Alice asked.

Doris shook her head. "I never got that impression. They seemed close, really supportive of each other."

Annie couldn't believe what she was hearing. "Did you meet Joan's ex-husband? Was he the reason Joan disappeared?"

"I don't know. Far as I know, he never came to the hospital," Doris said.

"You keep calling her Marie," Alice said. "We thought her name was Therese Marie."

Doris met Annie's gaze. "No. They had planned on naming the baby Therese Marie."

Annie took in a shallow breath. The stock certificates were intended for the baby.

"What happened to the baby?"

Doris shook her head. "I put Marie in touch with some adoption agencies in Portland. She left town. After that, I don't know."

"Thank you for coming to the hospital on your day off," Alice said.

"Anything we can do to help," Sarah said.

Doris added. "And now Joan came back after all these years and ... what a tragedy."

Annie shook her head. "It shocked us all."

Annie and Alice excused themselves and headed toward the lobby. "Do you suppose Joan's ex-husband is still around?" Alice asked.

"It seems he was the reason they came back here. He might have some answers." Annie pushed open the hospital doors.

"I can tell you right now, there are no Whitlocks in this area," said Alice.

"You said earlier that Joan might have gone back to her maiden name."

The two women walked across the parking lot. "In which case, we will never find him. He could have moved away or died by now. And we don't even know his name."

They were partway to the car when Annie's cell phone rang. "Hello."

"Annie, it's Ian." He took a deep breath. "I'm calling on behalf of the chief. Did you have any contact with Joan Whitlock before she died?"

"Yes, she came to my house looking for the stock certificates." Annie's neck muscles pinched tight. "I thought about calling the police, but I didn't know if it was warranted. She was just asking for something that belonged to her in the first place."

"Can you come down to the police station right away?" She'd never heard his voice sound so stressed.

～ 19 ～

*H*eading toward the police station, Annie was grateful that Alice was driving. Right now, she wasn't sure if she would be able to remember the directions. She was having trouble stringing two thoughts together. Why was Ian calling her to the police station? Obviously, she was probably the first person he had thought of when he saw that the dead woman was Joan Whitlock.

Annie spoke her thoughts out loud. "You don't think the police think I had something to do with Joan's death, do you?"

"Of course not." Fear strained Alice's voice as she offered Annie a forced smile.

Annie pressed her back against the seat when the town hall came into view.

Alice came to a stop and turned off the car. "Do you want me to come with you?"

Annie squared her shoulders to try to shake off the tension in her neck and back. "If they will let you."

"I'm sure they are not going to grill you under bright lights or anything." Alice sounded like she was trying to convince herself as well as Annie.

The two women got out of the car and entered the police station.

Ian came forward and grabbed Annie's hands. "Thank

you for coming so quickly. The chief has some questions he would like to ask you."

Chief Edwards, seated behind his desk, offered Annie a nod before rising to his feet. The broad-shouldered man was an intimidating figure. "Thanks for coming, Mrs. Dawson. Why don't you take a seat?"

Annie couldn't quite read the chief's expression. His features held a hardness that could be concern or suspicion. "Can my friend stay?" Her voice sound weak.

The chief narrowed his eyes but said, "Sure."

Ian squeezed Annie's shoulder. "Relax. We don't think you have done anything wrong."

Annie let out her breath. He must have seen the level of worry on her face. "I just thought maybe because I was the one who had contact with Joan ..."

"No," Ian managed a smile though it faded quickly.

Alice stepped forward. "So there was no foul play?"

"We didn't say that." Chief Edwards slammed a file down on his desk.

Annie's throat constricted. "You mean ... there was?"

The chief's glance bounced from Ian and then to Annie and Alice. He didn't have to say anything. Someone had killed Joan Whitlock. Annie reached over and grabbed Alice's hand, so grateful that her friend was with her.

"So why did you call me?"

The chief opened a drawer and pulled out a photograph. He pushed it across the desk toward Annie. "Is this the woman you met?"

Annie picked up the photograph and studied it. The picture was of a woman standing behind a white picket fence. The hair was a different color and not pulled back from her face, but it was the same woman she had met. "Yes, that is the woman who came to my door. Where did you get this photograph?"

"A friend of the dead woman sent it over to us," said the chief.

"A friend?" Still gripping the photograph, she turned slightly to face Ian. "I don't understand. What is going on? Why do you need me to identify her? The newspaper said it was Joan Whitlock." She set the photo back on the desk.

"That is what we initially thought. Everything in her possession identified her as Joan Whitlock. And then we got a call from the friend, a Marian Steffes over in Petersgrove."

"Petersgrove? I don't know where that is."

Alice seated herself in the chair beside Annie. "It's a little town. Really just a bump in the road—a few houses, a bar, and a post office. I did a party there a while ago."

"Marian said her friend didn't come home last night. She faxed us over that picture."

Annie wiggled in her seat as she absorbed what was being said. "And her friend's name isn't Joan Whitlock."

"Marian said her friend's name was *Janet Murray*," Ian said.

"Wait a second." Alice glanced nervously at Annie. "We think Joan might have changed her name. She was trying to hide her identity."

Ian paced a few feet and then picked up an envelope off the desk. "I went over to Linda Hunter's, because she said she thought she had a photo of the Joan who stayed at the Maplehurst." He pulled out the photograph and handed it to Annie. "This is what she gave me."

Annie grabbed the photo of "Janet" and looked at the two photos side by side. She gasped. The woman in the Maplehurst dining room was toward the front of the camera and in tight focus. Her dark hair was twisted up into an elegant bun. Gold jewelry set off the brightness in her eyes. Even though the picture of Janet was of her whole body and she was farther away from the camera, they were clearly two different women.

Numbness invaded Annie's limbs as she placed the photos back on the chief's desk.

The chief gathered up the photos. "Mrs. Dawson, I'll need to take a statement from you. Did the woman who came to your house give you any indication that someone might be after her?"

Annie shook her head. "She didn't say anything directly. It was just that … I had a feeling. Really, I was suspicious of her. But I didn't think she was in any danger." She looked Chief Edwards in the eye. "Maybe I should have come to you sooner."

Ian placed a supportive hand on Annie's shoulder. "You can't blame yourself. The chief wouldn't have been able to do much with a feeling."

The chief clicked on his computer. "We'll get through this interview as quickly as possible. Just try to remember exactly what she said to you."

The chief prompted her. Annie answered his questions as best she could. Ian and Alice both offered encouragement as she fought to bring out any detail that might help Chief Edwards. As she thought about her conversation with

Janet, she realized that the woman had given no indication that she was in danger. Annie's concerns had been over the woman's identity, that maybe she wasn't who she said she was. Her instincts had been right. Twenty minutes later, the chief thanked her and said they were done.

"Come on, ladies. Let me walk you outside," Ian offered.

The three of them stood in the parking lot. The confusion and the heartache overwhelmed Annie.

Ian sighed. "Here it is a beautiful sunny day, and we have to deal with such a suspicious tragedy."

"It's not stuff we want to think about, is it?" Annie sighed.

All the color had drained from Alice's face. Annie offered her a sideways hug. "Do you feel all right to drive?" Not that she felt any better.

Alice nodded. "I'll be OK. It's all so ... shocking."

The two women said goodbye to Ian and got into the Mustang.

Alice started the engine and shifted into reverse. "I don't know about you, but I could use a nice, long, head-clearing drive."

Annie leaned against the back of the seat. "That sounds like a great idea."

After putting the top down, Alice drove along the coastal road. Annie let the wind rustle her hair and enjoyed the feeling of the ocean breeze on her skin. Slowly her spirits lifted, and she could think straight again.

Alice brought the car to a stop in a gravel turnout to a remote part of the beach, and they got out. Huge boulders jutted out on the landscape between the shoreline and the turnout. To the west was an old-growth pine forest. Shadow and darkness blended with the bushy evergreens.

"I think there is a walking trail here somewhere if you want to go down to the shore." Alice pointed. "There." She trekked ahead on the narrow path.

Annie followed behind her friend, choosing her steps carefully on the rocky path. "I just realized something."

"What's that?" Alice spoke over her shoulder.

"The lady at Ocean Side Partners couldn't tell me who the stock was registered to. But I suspect Joan bought it. The real Joan could have just gone in and cashed her stock out—without the certificates—but something kept her from doing so. Janet posing as Joan didn't try to cash the stock in with her false I.D. For some reason, she wanted the actual stock certificates."

As the two women made their way closer to the shoreline, gulls dipped into the foamy waves. The breeze intensified.

"The only thing special about the stock certificates is that they were made out to Therese Marie, who we now know was the baby that Marie had here in Stony Point and gave up for adoption."

"How do we make all the pieces fit, Alice?" Annie stared out at the powerful waves cresting and smoothing as they reached the shore.

The rocky landscape died away, and they walked on a narrow band of sand.

"Maybe the real Joan is alive and well, and has been pulling the strings all along. She sends some guy in to try and find the certificates, and when that doesn't work, she sends in a Joan impersonator."

"What do we know about this Janet person?" Annie stopped walking. "What made her want to pretend to be Joan?"

Alice turned to face her, placing her hands on her hips. "We know where she lives. It's not that far a drive to Petersgrove."

"We should go there and ask around?"

The wind caught Alice's auburn hair and whipped it around. "You still feel responsible for what happened to her, don't you?"

"Partly yes, I keep thinking if I had gone to the police, things might have turned out differently."

Alice gathered her hair into her hands and held it tight. "What would you have told them? There was nothing illegal to report. Someone had come back for something that belonged to her."

Annie pressed her lips together. She played with the locket she had around her neck as a sadness rose up in her. "I know I can't bring Janet back, but I could at least figure out why she died."

"You have to stop beating yourself up." Alice's voice was filled with compassion.

"It would make me feel better to go over to Petersgrove, just to find out what kind of a person Janet was. If the real Joan put her up to this, we can always ask around if anyone saw the two of them together. I'm sure Linda would make another copy of the photograph of Joan."

"All right then. That's what we'll do," said Alice.

As they made their way back up the hill, Annie's cell phone rang.

"Annie, Wally here. I was hoping to get over to your

place to put the finishing touches on that library. I recut some of the scrollwork. We just need to secure it into place, and you can put those books back on the shelf. We can be over there in ten minutes."

"I'll be home to let you in, but then I've got some running around to do." Annie was out of breath from climbing back up the hill.

"That's fine. I can lock up when I leave," Wally said.

Alice agreed to drop Annie off. They could get the photo from Linda on the way out of town.

Only minutes after Annie stepped into Grey Gables, Wally and Douglas pulled up in Wally's car. Annie let them in and then ran a comb through her hair and refreshed her makeup before walking over to Alice's.

After stopping by the inn to get the photo of Joan from Linda Hunter, they headed inland to Petersgrove. In less than an hour they saw the welcome sign, followed by several houses spread far apart. "You were right when you said it wasn't much more than a bump in the road," Annie said.

"There are some surrounding farms that support the town." Alice slowed as she entered the village limits.

The main street had no stoplights and consisted of a post office, a drugstore that looked as if it also carried groceries, and a bar that advertised steak dinners for ten dollars.

Alice glanced from side to side. "So, inspector, where do we start?"

Annie peered out the window at the quaint cottages. "I suspect that this Janet was standing in her front yard when that picture was taken. There aren't that many houses around here."

"Gotcha," Alice said. "We drive through the neighborhood until we see the house."

Annie closed her eyes, trying to re-create the photo in her mind. "It was brick with a white fence."

The streets behind the business district were not more than three blocks long. Alice drove down one street and up another.

"There, on the corner," Annie pointed.

Alice brought the car to a stop in front of a brick house. "Now what?" Alice glanced over at her friend before opening the door.

"She must have neighbors. All we have to do is stand outside her house looking interested."

Alice shrugged. "It's your call, Miss Marple."

The two women got out of the car and walked up to the little house. The beds by the fence had all been prepared for planting. Tulips bloomed around the stairs that led up to the house. Shingles were missing from the roof of the house, and the trim needed a fresh coat of paint.

The curtains on the house next door moved; a moment later the front door opened. Annie elbowed Alice. "What did I tell you?"

An older woman dressed in a loose-fitting housecoat emerged and walked over to where the two of them stood. She shaded her eyes from the sun. "Are you looking for Janet?"

Annie stepped back from the fence. "Well, no, we heard the news ..."

The woman placed her palm on her chest. "Such a tragedy. I am the one who phoned the police over at Stony Point and faxed them the photograph."

"What made you think it was Janet and not Joan Whitlock, like the paper said?"

"The car in the newspaper article looked like Janet's. Weather permitting, Janet was out every morning working in her yard. She didn't come out this morning." The woman turned back toward her house. "I like to have my coffee on the porch. She always waved at me, and we had a few words."

The woman seemed more than willing to volunteer information without finding out if they were police or reporters. "What kind of person was Janet?"

"She bought the house and moved here about a year ago. From Augusta, I think. She was on some kind of disability, something to do with her heart."

Disability pay couldn't have provided Janet with much income. Maybe that was why the house was so run down. "Did she know a lot of people?"

The woman thought for a moment. "She never said anything about a husband, dead or alive. My George passed away just two years ago. Janet was a few years younger than me."

"Did she have visitors? Other people who might know something about her?"

"She said something about a son and daughter. I don't think they ever visited." The woman wrinkled up her face. "She kind of kept to herself, really. Nice enough lady, though. At the height of summer, her garden and flower beds were something to see." The woman leaned a little closer. "I can't garden anymore. Bursitis."

"I'm sorry to hear that." Alice's voice filled with sympathy toward the woman.

"Do you know why Janet would pretend to be somebody else?" Annie asked.

The woman rubbed a mole on her cheek. "That is bizarre, isn't it? I really can't tell you."

Annie pulled out the photograph of the real Joan. "Did you ever see her with this woman?"

The older woman studied the photograph and shook her head. "No, can't say as I ever have. Believe me, in a town this size, everyone would notice a stranger." Her eyes grew wide as though she remembered something. "I've got some muffins in the oven I need to get back to. You ladies have a nice day." She toddled up the sidewalk and into her house.

Once the woman was inside the house, Alice said, "That was a little too easy. She really wanted to talk. Although I don't know if she actually told us anything worthwhile."

"She told us plenty," Annie adjusted the strap of her purse on her shoulder. "She told us Janet was hurting for money, and she told us she was lonely. Either of those would be a motive for doing the little acting job that she did."

Alice's face shone with amazement. "My friend, you are a genius."

"She also told us that the real Joan never came around here." Annie checked her watch. "It's only two o'clock, but I am exhausted. I think a nice, quiet day at home would be the next thing on my agenda."

Annie and Alice took the short drive back to Stony Point. When Alice dropped Annie off at Grey Gables, the door was locked and Wally's truck was gone. A twinge of excitement zinged through her as she thought about the library finally being done.

Annie set her purse on the dining room table and walked to the library. Wally had done a beautiful job with the scrollwork. Like all good construction guys, the men had left a bit of a mess for Annie to clean up. Yes, it was broom clean, but bits and pieces of wood and sawdust were scattered across the floor, along with some discarded nails and screws.

She looked forward to straightening up the place. Using a little elbow grease was just what she needed to get her mind off of everything that had happened. Annie vacuumed and placed Gram's books back on the shelves. The final step was to pull the sheets off the furniture. After running her hand along the smooth wood of Grandpa's desk, she collapsed into Gram's chair. She plugged in the new lamp she'd gotten and arranged it so the light fell over the chair. This would be a fine room to spend hours in. She had enough outlets now so that she could set up a full desktop computer when she replaced her laptop.

A sense of satisfaction filled her. "Spiffy. Just spiffy."

Annie pulled from the shelf one of the classics she'd read as child and settled in. Hours later, when she finally looked up from her book, it had already begun to grow dark outside, and her stomach was growling.

A quiet day alone had been just what she needed to calm her troubled nerves. She walked down the hallway to the kitchen and checked the refrigerator for dinner possibilities. She pulled out yogurt and some lunch meat and cheese. Annie took a scoop of yogurt and licked off the spoon.

All Janet had to do was show up for that meeting at The Cup & Saucer to get the stock certificates. Janet would have had no way of knowing that Annie intended to grill her first. Annie set her spoon in the sink with a clatter as a realization hit her.

Janet had gotten cold feet, and that's why she'd been killed. That had to be it. Janet must have been paid or manipulated into playing Joan, and she had chickened out.

Annie grabbed the phone and dialed the police station. No one picked up. No doubt the chief was busy investigating. Annie waited for the beep and left a message. "Chief, this is Annie Dawson. I think I know why Janet was killed. Please give me a call back."

Annie drummed her fingers on the countertop. She grabbed the phone again and called Ian's cell.

Ian picked up on the second ring. "Hello there, Annie."

His voice always sounded so welcoming. He must have checked the number before he picked up. "Hi, Ian, I'm sorry to bother you."

"It's never a bother to hear from you."

Annie turned so she had a clear view of the window. Only a few stars spattered across the dark sky. "I know you can't tell me about the investigation, but I think I have come up with a plausible scenario."

"I'll pass your theory on to the chief. What is it?" Ian said.

"I think Janet was hired to impersonate Joan, and I think she—"

The phone went dead, and the lights went out. Annie stared at the ceiling for a moment. That mouse was at it again. She felt her way along the cupboards until her fingers touched the cold metal of a drawer handle. She opened the drawer and felt around for a flashlight.

With the flashlight in her hand, she made her way to the living room, sweeping her light around the room in search of her purse. She stumbled over the handbag that held the stock certificates. She propped it against the wall. After some searching, she located her purse on a side table and retrieved her cell phone.

Annie dialed Ian's number. His message clicked on. She tried Wally's number. Another message. But at least he hadn't let his cell go dead again. "Hi, Wally, it's Annie Dawson. It's about eight o'clock, and it looks like that mouse has chewed through some wires again. I don't have Douglas's phone number, and I am sitting here in the dark. So sorry to bother you."

Annie located another flashlight, set them both up in the kitchen, and put away some dishes and food. She placed her hands on her hips and studied the room shrouded in shadows. She could only do so much in the dark while she waited for Wally to return her call.

She retreated to the library with the flashlight and picked up the book she had been reading. If she angled the flashlight just right, she could see the words on the page. The windows in the library rattled, signaling an impending storm.

Annie couldn't concentrate. She checked her phone and contemplated calling Wally again. Ian might be wondering why they got cut off. Maybe she could try Wally's home phone. She'd have to look up the number. She was on her way to the kitchen to locate a phone book when someone knocked on the door.

Finally. Wally must have come right over without calling her back. Annie angled the flashlight down the hallway and walked toward the door. When she opened the door, Douglas stood with his arms crossed.

"Douglas. Did Wally send you?"

"Wally? Yeah, sure."

"Come on in. The lights have been out for at least forty minutes. I could survive the night without it. I could just go to bed, but I'm afraid all the food in the refrigerator will spoil. Do you think that mouse could have chewed on something again?" She handed him one of the flashlights.

Douglas followed her down the hallway as she talked. "Could be. Is the electricity out through the whole house?"

Annie's step faltered. "I think so. You know, last time it went out, it was only in certain rooms."

"Then it might be something different. Why don't I start with the breaker box?"

"You're the expert. A storm is brewing outside. Do you think that has anything to do with it?"

Douglas shrugged and flipped open the breaker box. Annie held her flashlight so it shone on the breakers. "If you don't mind." Douglas turned toward her so his face was out of the light. "I like to work alone."

Douglas's hostility caught her off guard. "I'm sorry. I was just trying to help." Annie took a step back. "I'll wait in the library. You guys did a nice job on it, by the way."

"Thanks." Shadows covered Douglas's face. She couldn't read his expression.

Feeling a bit put off, Annie retreated to the library and closed the door. Once again, she picked up the book she had been reading and collapsed into Gram's chair. After about ten minutes of sitting in the near darkness, she grabbed the flashlight and headed back toward the breaker box. There really was no reason for Douglas to be so abrupt. If he didn't apologize, she might have to tell Wally. Maybe he was one of those workers who was only on his best behavior when the boss was around.

When Annie got to the breaker box, Douglas was gone. She tilted her head and listened. Maybe he had gone up to the attic.

Annie made her way down the hall to the stairs. Seeing movement in her peripheral vision, she glanced into the living room. Had someone just been standing by the window?

Aiming the flashlight toward the window, she stepped into the living room. Annie shone the light all around, finding nothing. When she turned around, Douglas was standing on the other side of the couch.

Her breath caught. "What are you doing in here?"

"I wanted to check some outlets." His voice was low and husky.

She didn't know that much about electricity, but that didn't sound like the right way to get the electricity back on. "Oh, I see." She really needed to call Wally. She'd set her cell phone down on the way to get the phone book in the kitchen when Douglas had knocked on the door.

She returned to the library to retrace her steps, but then did an about-face. Maybe she had left it on the table by the front door. When she raced by the living room, she didn't see Douglas.

Annie scanned the flashlight across the table. Not there. She glanced out the window. Annie gripped the curtain she had been holding to one side. Douglas's van was parked outside. Her pulse drummed in her ears. The room seemed suddenly colder.

When she opened the front door to get a closer look at the van, a gust of wind hit her. Douglas's van was the same one that had followed her the first time she had put the stock certificates in the bank, and it was the same van that sped away the night Janet hadn't shown up at The Cup & Saucer.

Annie shut the door and turned around.

Douglas loomed over her. "Did you find what you were looking for?" His voice had taken on a threatening tone.

～ 20 ～

Annie pressed her back against the door. "I, um, I seem to have misplaced my phone. I think it might be in … in the kitchen." She moved to step past him, but he grabbed her arm at the elbow. "Excuse me," she said, trying to pull away.

He pressed his finger into her muscles. "I've lost something, too, and I think you know what it is."

Annie shook her head. "Please, let go of me."

He leaned close to her. His breath was hot on her ear. "I want those stock certificates."

Shock spread through her as she processed what Douglas had just said. "Are you … are you Joan's ex-husband?"

"That stock is mine. Joan was supposed to transfer it to me. She told me she would."

Annie stepped backward as Douglas talked. He stood between her and the door. "You're the one who broke into my house."

"Those are mine." He lunged toward her, and she darted away.

Annie turned and ran. As she ran, she grabbed the handbag and headed up the stairs. Douglas's footsteps pounded behind her. His hand gripped her leg. She fell on the stairs. His fingers pressed into her ankle. She screamed, kicked, and broke free.

Annie raced up to the landing. She pulled open the door to the attic and slipped the deadbolt in place before racing up the remaining stairs. Annie leaned over, out of breath. She gripped her knees. She could hear Douglas stomping up the stairs. He shook the attic door and groaned.

Even as she heard him stomping back down the stairs, she knew he wasn't going to give up that easily. He was probably locating a tool to open the door or knock it down. She glanced around the attic. What could she use to stop him?

The attic had only one exit, back down those stairs. Heart pounding, Annie raced around the room. Maybe there was another way out. If she could find a ladder or a rope, she might be able to climb out a window and down an outside wall.

Annie pushed a dresser across the top of the stairs. That would at least slow him down.

She flipped open one of the trunks and pulled out a sheet, ripping it with her teeth. She had just flipped open one of the tiny windows when she heard the stomping up the stairs. Then came a horrible banging on the door. He was going to break it down. Annie's fingers fumbled with the strips of torn sheet. She tied one strip to another like she'd seen in some movie.

"I only want what is rightfully mine. She promised me." He shouted through a crack in the door. He kept banging until he broke the wood. She heard the dead bolt slide out of place. She dropped the sheets, grabbed the handbag, and dove behind a stack of broken chairs.

As Douglas ran up the final flight of stairs, Annie pressed herself tighter into the dark corner.

She could see his feet as he shoved the dresser aside. He must have gone back to his van to get the wrench he held in his hand. His feet turned slowly. She held her breath.

He crossed the room. She heard him throwing boxes around. It was just a matter of time before he found her. Did she have time to get to the top of the stairs before he caught her?

She had to chance it. While he continued to toss boxes and furniture around, she crept out, staying close to the wall, crawling in the dark on all fours. She dragged the bag along. Then the room fell silent. A stack of boxes still hid her from view. Annie held her breath.

Douglas took two steps that seemed to echo in the stillness.

Annie burst out from behind the boxes and raced toward the stairs.

Douglas took big strides across the room and lunged toward her. He grabbed at the bag in her hand. She jerked it toward her. The bag split open, raining down stock certificates.

He grabbed one as it floated to the floor. The smile of satisfaction disappeared from his face as he held the flashlight on the certificate. "No!" He shook his head. "These were supposed to be made out to me!" Douglas's face turned red. And then he locked his gaze on Annie. His eyes were ice cold.

He intended to hurt her. She turned and raced down the attic stairs, falling into Ian's arms. In a whir of motion, she saw Chief Edwards slip past Ian and rush up the stairs. "Stop where you are!" He roared as he drew his gun.

"What does it matter anyway?" Defeat colored Douglas's words, and he held his hands up.

Annie trembled as Ian wrapped his arms around her. "How did you know to come?"

"At first when we got cut off, I thought maybe it was just the storm and that you would call back when you could, but then I got a feeling in here," he patted his chest, "that you were in danger."

Officer Peters thundered past them with his gun drawn.

"Why don't we get you downstairs?" Ian guided Annie down to the living room. Outside, she saw the flashing lights of two police cars.

Annie slumped down onto the couch. "My heart is still racing. That was enough excitement to last a lifetime." The room was still dark. She had dropped her flashlight in the attic.

Ian found a candle on a nearby table, lit it, and set it on the coffee table. "Now. Tell me what happened?"

"Douglas is Joan's ex-husband. He thought the stock had been made out to him. I think if the stock was still listed in Joan's name at Ocean Side, showing the actual certificates with his name written on them might have been the leverage he needed to cash them in."

The police brought Douglas down the stairs in handcuffs. Even in the dim light, Annie could see that his expression was filled with venom. Just as the police opened the door, Wally stepped inside. He briefly stared at Douglas and shook his head as the police shoved Douglas out the front door. Wally then rushed over to Annie.

"What is going on, Annie? I came as soon as I got the message."

"It's a long story. Douglas came into the house to take the stock certificates."

"What in the world?" Wally rubbed his dark curly hair as though he was trying to absorb what Annie had told him. "That's why he asked me to hire him! He must have taken my key and made a copy of it."

Annie wrapped her arms around herself. She still hadn't calmed down from all of the excitement. "Douglas must have messed with something outside the house to make the electricity go out."

"I'll go have a look. It's the least I can do." Wally shuffled from one foot to the other. "I feel real bad."

"You had no way of knowing, Wally," Annie said.

"I'll go see what I can do." Wally left through the front door. "He probably cut the lock on the access panel and yanked a connector out."

Annie leaned forward, resting her hands on her knees. "What a night."

"It's all over now," Ian comforted.

Annie sat up straight. "But it isn't over, Ian. We still don't know what happened to Joan Whitlock."

"Do you think we'll ever know?"

Annie shook her head. "Well, Douglas might talk. He must have talked Janet into doing her Joan impersonation. Maybe he promised her some shares of the stock, and he played on her loneliness. That means he was probably the one who ..." Annie closed her eyes and rested her head against the back of the couch. She shuddered. This was all too much.

Ian rose to his feet. "You've been through a lot. Are you going to be OK?"

Annie sighed. Her heartbeat had returned to normal, and her hands weren't shaking anymore. "I'll be fine ... in time. Knowing that Douglas is in a jail cell goes a long way toward helping me find a little peace."

Ian draped his hand over Annie's. "You are one brave lady, Annie Dawson."

A sense of gratitude spread through her. "I'm so glad you acted on that impulse to come over." Her recovery would have been a lot slower if he hadn't shown up, and she might not have survived the ordeal at all.

After Annie said goodbye to Ian, she waited for Wally to get the electricity going before trudging up the stairs. Now that the excitement had worn off, she realized how exhausted she was. She fell into bed and was already drifting off when Boots jumped up and settled at her feet.

～ 21 ～

The next day Annie got to work cleaning up the disarray and gathering up the certificates that had been scattered all over the attic floor. She stared at the one with the handwritten name Therese Marie Gilkerson. Her hand brushed over the piece of paper. This had to be Joan's handwriting. Joan had intended to give a gift to her granddaughter. Not only had she never been able to give the gift, but she had also lost her granddaughter. Annie gathered the rest of the certificates into a tidy pile. She knew she had to let go of the idea of finding Joan. She had to close this chapter of her life.

Coming down from the attic, Annie removed her rubber gloves. She hoped the excitement had frightened away the mice. After a quick shower, she went downstairs to pour herself a cup of coffee. She found herself on the porch, holding the warm cup and looking out at the ocean. A sense of restlessness filled her as she studied the winding path that led through tall windblown grass to a rocky shoreline. Far in the distance, waves came to a foamy white peak.

When she had found the stock certificates, she had pictured a happy ending: She would find Joan and return the stocks, so Joan could give them to Therese. So simple.

"Not everything wraps itself into a beautiful package with a tidy bow," she whispered.

Inside, the phone rang, and Annie ran to answer it. "Annie," Ian's warm tenor voice came across the line. "How are you doing this morning?"

"Better than last night. I guess I'm still a little frazzled by everything that's happened."

"Listen, I wanted to give you the news before it hits the television and afternoon papers. It will at least be a regional story."

"Yes?"

"Last night Douglas Emery confessed to killing Janet for the exact reasons that you suspected. The chief said it was OK if I told you, but I would appreciate it if you would keep a lid on it."

Annie gripped the phone a little tighter. "Did Douglas say anything about what happened to the real Joan?"

"No, he hasn't said anything. I just thought you should know about the confession ahead of time. Reporters might be coming by to ask you questions as soon as the story breaks."

Facing a barrage of questions and reliving Douglas's attack was the last thing she wanted to do. "Thanks, Ian. I'll just have to make myself scarce." She knew exactly where she would hide. Annie got her things together and headed for A Stitch in Time. As she turned on Maple Street, she thought about the news Ian had given her. If Douglas was capable of killing one woman in rage, could he have done the same to Joan?

Annie entered A Stitch in Time. Just seeing Mary Beth behind the counter made her less anxious. This store had such a familiar and welcoming feel to it.

Mary Beth looked up from her paperwork. "I heard you

had a little excitement last night ... another break-in."

The Stony Point rumor mill was already turning. "Yes, and now I am hiding. Ian thinks that this story will go regional. I just don't have the energy to deal with reporters' questions right now."

"Your secret is safe with me. You are welcome to hide out all day if you like." Mary Beth's response confirmed what Annie had thought all along. Mary Beth's tendency to talk about other people's problems wasn't out of a desire to gossip, but because she cared about people. Mary Beth would respect her need for privacy. She was glad, too, that Mary Beth hadn't pressed her about why a break-in would be a big news story, so she could keep Douglas's confession under wraps.

"Is Kate here today?" Annie wandered around the store.

"She has the day off," Mary Beth said.

Annie picked up some tangerine yarn. "I think I am done with layettes for a while. I'm going to start on an afghan." Annie selected some yarns in bright spring colors and found a chair by the window. She had been working for about half an hour when Alice burst through the door.

"What is up with the big Portland news truck outside your house?"

"And good afternoon to you too," said Annie. If the news trucks were showing up, reporters must have gotten wind of Douglas's confession.

Alice took a seat beside her friend. "Sorry. There was a small thing in the police report about a man being arrested for breaking into a house on Ocean Drive. Is there something more to the story?"

Mary Beth rearranged the pattern books. "Annie is hiding out right now."

"You're welcome to hide with me if you like," Annie said as she created a row of popcorn stitches.

Alice unzipped her handbag. "As a matter of fact, I did bring my cross-stitch with me."

The two women worked in silence. Mary Beth put on a light instrumental CD. Annie enjoyed the feel of the sun streaming through the window and the good company.

Mary Beth returned from the storeroom and placed a box on the counter. "Estelle from Seaside came into the store yesterday. She sure would love to see all the women get together a couple of times a year."

"Ian said that it would be nice if we made the gift to the hospital an annual event." Annie placed her crochet work in her lap.

"Having a few get-togethers throughout the year would help ensure that we could pull off another project like that," Alice added.

Annie took in a deep breath. "Doing another project like that sounds wonderful."

"And next year, we might have a new batch of teenagers." Mary Beth opened the box of new inventory.

"With Janet's death and everything that happened, I didn't even have time to read the article about the dedication ceremony."

"I saved the article." Mary Beth skirted around to the other side of the counter and bent down. A moment later she popped her head up, holding a newspaper. "I thought it would be nice to get it framed and hang it up in the shop.

I bought several copies."

"Everything has been such a whirlwind. I don't even know where I put my copy of the newspaper." Annie rose from her seat. She took the newspaper, avoiding looking at the cover story.

"You can take one of my copies," Mary Beth offered.

Annie flipped through the pages until she came to the full-page article. The reporter had taken half a dozen pictures. One picture of Taylor and Lily with Viola was particularly striking. The woman was sandwiched between the two girls, their heads pressed close together, all of them beaming.

Mary Beth winked at her. "You done good, kid."

Alice pulled her thread through the cloth. "I think you have started a Stony Point tradition. Think of it, Annie, after you and I are gone, this tradition will live on."

That idea appealed to her. A legacy of sorts. Just like Gram. Annie grabbed a scissors off the counter and cut the article out. "I don't want to keep the whole paper, just this article."

The women worked for several more hours. Business at the store was slow, with only a few customers. Annie didn't recognize any of them, probably tourists. No danger of anyone letting the cat out of the bag and giving up her hiding place.

Annie held up the afghan she had started, pleased with her progress. "Do you suppose the newspeople are gone from Grey Gables by now?"

Alice checked her watch. "If you like, I can go back and be a spy for you. I'll call you with a report."

"Thanks."

Alice left the shop. Ten minutes later, Annie rose to her feet. "I think I might need to stretch my legs. Thanks for letting me hide out."

"Anytime," said Mary Beth.

Annie had just stepped out onto the sidewalk when her cell phone rang.

"Agent Zero Zero, reporting in." Alice's exuberant voice came across the line.

Annie laughed. "How does it look on your end, Agent Zero Zero?"

"The Portland truck is gone, but there is another one here. I can't tell where it is from," Alice said.

"They can't stay there forever. They have got to leave pretty soon to go do their evening news, don't they?"

"That is what I was thinking. What do you say I treat you to either a late lunch or an early dinner, whatever you want to call it, at the Grand Avenue Fish House? They should be gone by the time we get done eating."

"That sounds like a plan. I'll meet you there." Annie snapped her phone shut and headed to her car.

Since it was between the lunch and dinner hour, Annie and Alice enjoyed a nice quiet meal with great service. Only one other table in the entire restaurant was occupied.

"We seem to be making a habit of eating out when nobody else is." Annie took a bite of her shrimp fettuccine. She pulled the article about the ceremony out of her purse and unfolded it.

"It's a nice article, isn't it?" Alice dipped her lobster in butter.

"Yes, the reporter did a great job of getting pictures of everyone involved."

The women finished up dinner.

Alice put her napkin on the table. "Tell you what. Since we came in separate cars, why don't I drive by the house and let you know if the reporters are gone."

Annie shook her head. "What would I do without you?"

While Annie waited for news from Alice, she walked out on the pier, hoping to enjoy the coolness of the evening. Something niggled at the back of her mind. Something she couldn't quite put her finger on. The water was relatively calm tonight. The waves lapping against the shore created a comforting rhythm as the evening light waned.

Her cell phone rang.

"It's all clear." Alice seemed to be enjoying playing lookout.

"Thanks, Alice." Annie drove home, unlocked her door, and stepped inside Grey Gables. It was still early enough that she could work some more on her afghan. She chose the library. Adding an outlet allowed her to have an additional lamp, which made it bright enough to see the details on her tiny stitches.

She worked until nearly ten o'clock, enjoying the comfort of Gram's chair with Boots curled at her feet and the memories that flowed anytime she sat in this room. But as Annie went up to bed, she felt a sense of emptiness she couldn't explain. Something felt incomplete. She couldn't let go of the idea that there was some connection she needed to make to create a sense of finality.

～ 22 ～

The next morning Annie was in the kitchen drinking coffee and watching a hummingbird flit around her flowers when the doorbell rang.

She had counted on some intrepid reporter returning to get a statement from her. Today she felt ready to deal with the press. Annie walked down the hallway into the living room and swung the door open.

No news trucks were parked in her driveway, but a beige sedan was. Annie stared at the woman standing on her porch. The key ring she held indicated that her car was a rental. She was older, dressed stylishly in a royal blue pantsuit. Her red-leather handbag matched the red polish on her nails. Her gray hair fell in soft curls around her face. Her brown eyes revealed a sharpness that suggested intelligence.

Maybe the woman worked for a newspaper, not a television station. "Are you a reporter?"

The woman ignored her question. "Please forgive me for bothering you at such an early hour. I took the first flight out from Montreal and drove from Portland."

Annie took a step back, feeling suddenly leery of the stranger. If she was a reporter, she didn't act like it. "What is this about?"

"There is no easy way to say this." The woman squared her shoulders. "I'm Joan Whitlock."

Annie shook her head. Not this again. She started to close the door, but something stopped her.

The woman spoke calmly, as though responding to the inner turmoil her announcement had created for Annie. "I know this is a shock. And after what has happened to you, I don't expect you to believe me. Even saying the name feels strange to me. You see, I haven't been Joan Whitlock for years. I don't have anything that could prove that I am Joan Whitlock."

The woman's calm demeanor kept Annie from closing the door. "Why are you back here now?"

"I've been living in Canada under a different name. We get some American stations up there, so I saw the news stories. I recognized Grey Gables. I am so sorry about your grandmother. She was a very special lady to me."

Annie went numb, struggling to absorb what this woman was saying. "Why didn't you come back sooner for those stock certificates?" Maybe Janet wouldn't be dead.

"When I saw that Douglas was in jail, I knew it was finally safe to return." An undercurrent of pain colored Joan's voice when she spoke about Douglas.

Annie studied the woman in front of her. The defensiveness she had felt faded. "I'm sorry I was so abrupt." Her instincts told her that this woman was who she said she was. "Do you want to come in and sit down and tell me the rest of this story? I'm dying to hear it."

"I would be delighted." Joan found a seat on the couch in the living room, and Annie took a chair opposite her.

"I know some of your story already. You came into town all those years ago with your pregnant daughter."

"Douglas lived in Petersgrove. With Marie's husband gone, I thought maybe Douglas would step up and be a father to his daughter and grandfather to the baby. I hadn't seen him in years, and I guess I was hopeful he had changed. But he was worse than ever. His electrician business had gone under. He was an angry man when we were married and doing well, but now that his bad choices had left him financially destitute, he was much worse."

A sense of compassion filled Annie for what Joan must have endured. "All these years, Douglas thought those stock certificates were made out to him."

Joan folded her hands in her lap. "I told him they were. Because he made me so afraid, I would say anything to keep him from getting angry at me."

"Why run away? Why change your identity?"

"Marie had married and moved away. Douglas was wild. He threatened me. I was afraid for my life. So I left Stony Point to finalize my disappearing act. Then when Marie was expecting the baby and her husband died, we reunited in Stony Point. But she was in no condition to travel so I left her here, intending to come back for her. But I was afraid for her. I was afraid for the baby. I didn't contact my daughter for years, because if Douglas found out I was alive, he would come after both of us."

"But you did get in touch with her eventually. She came back here for the stock certificates."

"No, it was never about the stock certificates—not for me, anyway. Douglas thought if he could find the actual stock certificates with his name handwritten on them, he would have the legal leverage to cash them in. And I wasn't

Joan Whitlock anymore. I couldn't cash them in."

"So why did your daughter return to Stony Point?"

Joan lifted her chin and took a breath. "Marie came back to see if she could find out what happened to her daughter." Joan hesitated for a moment. She spoke slowly, each word being painful to utter. "She had found out that the adoption agency in Portland had placed Therese with a family in Stony Point. She wasn't going to cause trouble. She just wanted to see her."

"But something happened," Annie said.

"She must have run into Douglas in town. The accident report said she was driving very fast. She must have been terrified."

Annie leaned forward and rested her hand on Joan's. "I'm so sorry. You've suffered so much loss."

"It hasn't been easy."

"And Gram wanted to help you." Annie's throat had grown tight with emotion. What this poor woman must have gone through to lose both her daughter and her grand-daughter.

Joan sighed. "Your grandmother was such a support during a really hard time. I didn't want to have the stock certificates with me. Douglas was stalking me."

As Joan talked, a realization spread through Annie. The final piece of the puzzle fell into place. "But he's in jail now. You are safe."

"Yes, I can be Joan Whitlock again. All those years ago, I thought things were going to go differently. I was going to take care of things in New Hampshire so Douglas wouldn't be able to find me, and then I would come back for my daughter and her baby, and retrieve the stock certificates from your grandmother. The three of us would have a nice life together." She looked up, tears rimming her eyes.

"I can't bring your daughter back, but there is something I might be able to do," said Annie. "I'll have to make some phone calls. Can you come by A Stitch in Time at about five o'clock on Wednesday? I know that means you'll have to stay in town."

"I don't mind."

"I'll let you know if I can't pull things together, or if I'm wrong about a hunch I have."

Annie offered Joan a hug at the door and then raced to the phone. She called Mary Beth at the store.

"Mary Beth, I am not going to make our Hook and Needle Club meeting today, but it's for a good reason."

"Oh, we will miss you. You have had so much excitement in the last few days. I am sure the ladies are hoping to be filled in."

"I know. We'll just have to do a twice-a-week thing and get together some other day this week."

"I bet the ladies would love that."

Annie hung up the phone and got to work.

~ 23 ~

The teen class was just wrapping up when Annie arrived at A Stitch in Time on Wednesday. A sense of anticipation threaded through her as she waited. She smiled at Erin, Mackenzie, and Vanessa.

Erin offered her an impulsive hug. "Thank you for everything. I'm going to be a volunteer at both the hospital and at Seaside."

She brushed a strand of Erin's hair behind her ear. "It was my pleasure to be a part of the class. I'm sure I will be dropping in from time to time, especially as we get ready to do another hospital project."

Even though the class had officially broken up and most of the teens had left, Lily and Taylor continued chatting as they worked on their projects.

Lily's mother came into the store and offered Annie a knowing glance.

"Lily, I have a surprise for you," Annie said. "I spoke to your mother earlier, and I have her permission." She'd spent most of Tuesday talking to nurses and working with Lily's mother to get records.

Lily's gaze darted around the room. A nervous smile graced her face. "I hope this is good."

"Yes, it's good," said Lily's mother.

"Can Taylor stay with me? She's my friend."

"Sure."

Joan stepped into the shop. She was dressed stylishly as always, but a look of anxiety clouded her expression. "I'm here," she said softly.

Annie didn't say anything. She only turned slightly to direct Joan's attention to Lily sitting in the chair, holding her knitting.

Joan let out a gasp.

A look of confusion crossed Lily's face.

Annie had seen the resemblance the moment she put the photograph of the younger Joan beside the newspaper photo of Lily. "Lily, this is your Grandmother Joan."

"My grandma. You mean—?" She stood up.

Joan held trembling fingers to her mouth. "You are so beautiful. Lily is just the perfect name for you."

Lily's mother Karen stepped toward her daughter. "I always longed for you to have an extended family and to know where you came from."

Taylor rose to her feet. "Hey, Lily, this is so cool. You have a grandma."

Slowly, hesitantly, Lily stepped toward Joan. Joan held out her arms, and Lily stepped into her embrace.

"I know this is all kind of sudden for you," said Joan. "But not a day has gone by that I didn't think about you and pray for you."

Lily stepped free of the hug. "Really?"

"I was thinking of you before you were born." Joan pulled one of the stock certificates out of her purse. "Your mom and I were going to call you Therese Marie, but I like Lily."

Lily stared at the stock certificate. "What's this?"